Redefining Lines

Book One of the Lines Duet

S. BRIANNE

TIMEBACK PUBLISHING

Redefining Lines

Book One of the Lines Duet

Published by Timeback Publishing

ISBN 979-8-9992096-0-3 (eBook)

ISBN 979-8-9992096-1-0 (Print)

To my mother.

The reader who raised me, the believer who backed me, and the heart behind every adventure I've ever dared to take.

To my readers.

May the best stories linger in your minds, and may a few be brave enough to find their way onto your pages, too.

Prologue

SUMMER '99

CHALK DUST SWIRLED THROUGH the golden afternoon light, settling on empty notebooks and sweaty palms. The classroom hummed with whispers and the scratch of pencils. Unfamiliar faces turned toward Sutton like curious museum exhibits, studying the new arrival.

"Sutton?"

The substitute's voice floated above the rustle of paper, tentative and unsure.

Sutton raised her hand slowly. Thirty pairs of eyes flicked toward her. Her heart pounded against her ribs, blood rushing in her ears. Only the second day of third grade, and already the walls felt like they were closing in.

They'd left Maine for Dad's "can't-miss opportunity," which had become Mom's mantra while they packed their life into cardboard boxes. Sutton had slammed her bedroom door so hard the hinges rattled, stomped until the floorboards protested. But eventually, hunger pulled her out, the smell of Mom's lasagna too strong to resist. Weeks later, morning dew shimmered on their For Sale sign, and the highway stretched endlessly west.

Fractions crawled across the blackboard now, but Sutton's mind wandered. She tugged at a loose thread on her blue leggings, watching it unravel as her life had. The oversized denim jacket weighed heavily on her shoulders. Around her, kids in neon T-shirts laughed too loudly, moved too fast, existed too easily.

When the lunch bell rang, the room erupted. Sutton unzipped her backpack and pulled out her brown paper bag. She chose a quiet spot by the trash can, the sour smell of milk cartons mixing with peanut butter and jelly. The sandwich stuck to the roof of her mouth, tasting like cardboard and homesickness. She left it half-eaten and slipped outside.

The playground smelled of sun-baked asphalt and freshly cut grass. Sutton leaned against the rough bark of an elm, its shadow cool against her back. She opened her dog-eared *Charlie and the Chocolate Factory*, disappearing into Wonka's world. Day after day passed like this. Silent. Solitary. Endless.

Until today.

"Stop it!"

The shout split the air like a crack of thunder.

A girl with hair like spun honey stood her ground, cheeks flushed as she shoved a boy backward. He stumbled, fists clenching. No adults in sight.

Something sparked in Sutton's chest, a sudden, fierce heat. Her book hit the ground as her sneakers carried her forward.

The boy glared. "What are you looking at?" His voice cracked mid-sentence.

"Leave her alone."

Her voice sounded foreign in her own ears.

The boy hesitated, muttered something, then backed off.

The girl brushed grit from her scraped knees and gave Sutton a small, shaky smile.

"Thanks."

Sutton sat beside her, the pavement still warm through her jeans.

"I'm Brynn," the girl said, waving a hand with chipped purple nail polish.

"Sutton."

They smiled at each other.

"Why was he being mean to you?" Sutton asked.

Brynn shrugged, a small grin breaking through.

"Tyler enjoys being the center of attention."

Light and unexpected laughter slipped out of both of them.

The bell rang, sending everyone back inside. Brynn stood, brushing dust from her shorts.

"See you around?"

Sutton nodded.

For the first time in six long weeks, the world felt bigger than her loneliness. And in the cracks of the blacktop, friendship quietly took root.

One

Sutton unlocked the door to her New York apartment, and a wave of spiced air hit her. It was her favorite time of year.

Soft light from the living room spilled into the hallway, the twinkle of her tree casting a kaleidoscope of color across the walls. A golden star crowned the top, its edges catching the glow like a warm halo. Garland dusted with fairy lights wound around the mantel and picture frames, filling the space with pine and nostalgia, memories of snow days, hot cocoa, and her parents' laughter.

She closed her eyes for a moment, breathing it in as if she could bottle the feeling.

But tonight, nostalgia would have to wait.

Sutton kicked off her heels with a soft clack against the hardwood and hurried toward her bedroom. The lateness of the hour gnawed at her; she was always running behind, always chasing some invisible clock. Peeling off her blouse, she slipped into black tights and ankle boots, then tugged on one of her go-to Alice + Olivia dresses, the one that hugged her in all the right places.

She twirled once in the mirror, the fabric catching the glow of the bedside lamp.

“Good enough,” she murmured.

A glance at the clock made her pulse tick faster. Purse in hand, she flew out the door, the soft glow of the tree following her into the night.

***

“You’re late,” Brynn teased as Sutton slid into the booth, her cheeks flushed from the cold.

“Yes, but I come in style.”

Sutton tilted her chin and swept a hand down her dress like a game-show hostess.

Brynn laughed, shaking her head.

“Some things never change.”

Outside, the city was a blur of brake lights and snowflakes, but inside the restaurant, candles flickered and glasses clinked in a rhythm that felt timeless. It was one of those rare nights that slowed the world down, just the two of them again, made possible only because Brynn happened to be in New York for work.

Brynn rubbed her hands together, the chill of winter still clinging to her skin. As a publicist, her life revolved around press tours, red carpets, and crisis management. What she missed most were nights like this.

"This city's making me soft. I forgot how brutal December could be."

"Los Angeles has you spoiled," Sutton said, unfolding her napkin. "Too much sunshine makes you weak."

Brynn smirked. "Maybe. Or maybe I've just grown. Why battle the cold when I can sip margaritas on a beach in December? But there's something about New York at Christmas with the chaos, the lights, the street noise. It's magic. Messy, loud, perfect magic."

Sutton smiled, holding up her glass.

"I missed this."

"Me too," Brynn said softly.

For a moment, the quiet between them felt easy, familiar.

Then Brynn perked up, sliding her phone across the table.

"Speaking of missing things."

Sutton groaned when she saw the name flashing on the screen: *Alexander.*

"You didn't."

Brynn's grin was shameless.

"Relax. I didn't."

Their dynamic had always been a high-wire act, chaotic but addictive.

"But the sex is just..." Brynn leaned closer and lowered her voice. "...so us."

Sutton raised her glass.

"To great sex. Always worth a toast."

Brynn laughed, shaking her head.

"You're terrible."

"I'm honest." Sutton grinned. "Anyway, what's new with you?"

Brynn's fingers drummed against the table.

"The trip's almost here. I can't wait to ditch deadlines and small talk. Just snow, mulled wine, and Marcus trying to use that damn hot tub even when it's twenty degrees out."

Sutton chuckled.

"Tradition. You have to respect the commitment."

Brynn's smile shifted, playful but a little hesitant.

"Also, I forgot to tell you, I invited someone new this year."

Sutton raised an eyebrow.

"Define 'someone.'"

"Wesley," Brynn said, as if it were casual.

Sutton blinked.

"Wesley?"

"You know, Wesley Preskott. The singer."

Sutton sifted through faint memories of headlines and viral clips.

"Is he the one who sang that moody breakup anthem?"

"*Heartstrings,*" Brynn supplied. "Or *Lost at Midnight.* Read TMZ occasionally, please."

Recognition clicked.

"Right, him." Sutton crossed her arms. "So he's gracing us mortals with his pop-star presence? Should I curtsy or just faint?"

Brynn rolled her eyes, but her voice softened.

"He's had a rough year."

Sutton tilted her head.

"Burnout?"

"Worse. He told me after a show that he felt completely disconnected, like he was performing for thousands of people but couldn't feel any of it. Said the stage used to feel like home. Now it's just noise."

Sutton frowned, quiet now.

"He walked off a sold-out tour," Brynn continued. "Told his manager he needed time off, or he'd lose himself completely."

"Damn," Sutton said softly.

"I think he's still figuring out who he is offstage. So I invited him. No cameras, no pressure. Just snow, friends, and peace."

"Isn't he, like, twenty?" Sutton teased.

"Twenty-five. And don't worry, he's not bunking with you." Brynn smirked. "It'll be good for him. Everyone needs a reset, even the ones with tour buses and fan mail."

Sutton exhaled, a smile tugging at her lips.

"The more, the merrier."

Two

When Sutton arrived at Brynn's cabin, the satisfying click of the lock welcomed her home. She dropped her luggage just inside the doorway, excitement and memory wrapping around her like the winters they'd shared before.

But there was no time to linger.

She stepped back outside, her breath fogging in the cold, and hurried toward Tati's, the dimly lit Spanish tapas spot that had become a ritual for their group. The winter chill nipped at her cheeks, but anticipation kept her warm as she crossed the snowy path.

The moment Sutton stepped onto Tati's patio, the world seemed to exhale. The space glowed like a hidden oasis. Delicate white lights wove between low-hanging branches, radiant heaters pushed back the cold, and candlelight flickered across tables like tiny dancing flames. Plush throws draped over chair backs invited guests to lean in and stay a while.

Her eyes landed on their usual table beneath the most elaborately decorated tree.

Marcus was mid-story, gesturing wildly as Peter rolled his eyes with practiced patience. Zoe and Cassie were doubled over in laughter, clearly sharing a private joke.

Brynn spotted her first, lighting up like a sparkler.

"There she is!"

Soft cheers rose from the table as Sutton approached, each hug stitching her back into the fabric of their shared history.

Marcus and Brynn had grown up in neighboring vacation homes; their friendship was as sturdy as old roots. Five years ago, they'd begun co-hosting this annual winter trip, and the tradition had stuck. Peter, Zoe, and Cassie came through Marcus, each different, each essential. Sutton and Everett had joined through Brynn, rounding out what eventually became *The Original Seven.*

Between summers, holidays, and these yearly cabin retreats, the group became a kind of chosen family. Careers and cities could scatter them, but this trip remained the anchor that pulled everyone back together.

Once Sutton finished hugging the usual crew, Brynn slipped an arm around her shoulder and steered her toward a free seat.

"Sutton, meet Wesley. Wesley, Sutton," Brynn said casually.

Wesley sat across the table, his presence quiet but unmistakable. He stood, extending his hand with a warm, open smile.

"Nice to meet you," Sutton said, polite and a touch guarded.

His smile held steady as he took her hand.

"Nice to meet you too," he said, his voice low and unhurried.

Her first impression hit quickly: sharp jawline, tousled dark hair, expressive eyes that hinted at stories he didn't say out loud. But it was the smile, softening the intensity in his gaze, that caught her off guard. It felt human. Not celebrity-polished. Just real.

If she were younger, she might've teased him and let her eyes linger. But Sutton was older, wiser. She didn't entertain stories built on happenstance and charm, not anymore.

Brynn clapped her hands together, breaking the moment.

"Alright! Now that we're all here, drinks."

The night unfolded with laughter, shared stories, and the clink of wine glasses. The strain of Sutton's long drive eased as the table warmed around her, the conversation seamless and comforting.

Wesley mostly watched, absorbing the group with quiet attentiveness. They fit together with the ease of people whose lives had intertwined over the years.

Marcus's theatrical storytelling commanded the table. Brynn matched him step for step, their banter an unspoken language. Zoe and Cassie exchanged looks and giggled like conspirators. Peter chimed in with perfectly timed sarcasm, each remark a well-placed punctuation mark.

And Sutton.

Wesley's gaze kept drifting to her, lingering longer than he meant. She didn't compete for attention; she didn't need to. Her presence was grounded. She listened with genuine interest, her eyes bright and thoughtful. And when she laughed, it was a soft but full sound, like she meant it.

For a moment, just a moment, Wesley felt a quiet ache of envy.

For all his fame, his world was small. Conversations were transactional: promos, schedules, interviews. His days were noise; his nights were empty.

But here, laughter moved freely. Warmth wasn't a performance. People were connected in ways he had forgotten were possible.

Still, he felt like the new kid at a lunch table. Not unwelcome, just not woven in. Not yet.

He leaned back, letting the group's rhythm wash over him.

Across the table, Brynn caught his eye and winked.

See? the look seemed to say. *This is what you've been missing.*

For the first time in a long while, Wesley let himself believe it.

Here, no one cared about his fame or his failures.

Here, he could just be Wesley.

Three

The next day unfolded beneath a crisp winter sky, a soft haze settling over the snow-covered landscape. By late afternoon, the sinking sun painted everything in lavender and gold, the colors bleeding into one another like watercolors on cold paper.

Sutton padded down the stairs to Brynn's kitchen, her skin still warm from a long shower. The house was hushed, a welcome contrast to the vibrant buzz the night before. She hadn't seen Brynn or Wesley since they'd returned early from snowboarding. After her own snowshoe trek and a quiet stop at the coffee shop, she'd opted to cocoon herself in solitude.

She moved easily in the kitchen, hands busy but mind clear. The refrigerator hummed softly; oil sizzled in a pan; the world felt steady again. She poured herself a glass of wine and let the velvety red swirl before taking a slow sip. The quiet wrapped around her like a familiar sweater.

The stillness was bliss.

Until keys jingled and the front door creaked open.

Sutton turned, fingers still curled around her wineglass. Wesley stepped inside, hair tousled from the cold, cheeks flushed pink. He looked surprised to see her.

"Oh, hey," he said. "I didn't realize anyone was here. I just came back to grab Peter's ski jacket from my car."

"Not at all," Sutton said, her smile easy, though something fluttered under her ribs. "Quiet night in. The others went to Lazarus?"

Wesley nodded, his gaze drifting toward the stove, the scent of roasted chicken and fennel pulling him in.

"That smells amazing."

"Thanks." She gave the pot a quick stir. "I made too much, as usual."

A beat of silence stretched between them. Not awkward, just unfamiliar.

"I'd invite you to stay," Sutton added with a light laugh, "but it's nothing exciting. Just me and dinner."

It was the kind of polite offer you didn't expect anyone to take.

But Wesley blinked, surprised.

"Well." He let out a breath, "honestly, I wasn't feeling up for going out tonight either."

Sutton raised an eyebrow.

"Really? I figured you'd be where all the fun is."

He laughed softly, a self-aware sound.

"Trust me, I'm not always the *fun crowd* guy. Besides, you're underselling this whole quiet-night-in thing."

A faint warmth crept up her neck. "Well, I can't promise the food is better than Lazarus."

"If it tastes half as good as it smells," he said, sincerity slipping through, "and you don't mind the company."

She hesitated only a moment before waving him in.

"Sure. Would you like a glass of red?"

Wesley settled against the counter as she handed him a wineglass. His shoulders eased; the room shifted, the air warming around them.

"Honestly," Sutton said, checking the chicken, "I didn't take you for the low-key dinner type."

"That's probably because you know very little about me."

"I know some things," she teased. "Tabloid things."

Wesley groaned dramatically.

"Okay, well, don't trust all that. According to the internet, I'm dating three people and hate my band. Meanwhile, we just argued once about snacks on the tour bus."

Sutton's laugh bubbled out, unguarded.

"Noted. And the dating three people part?"

Wesley smirked.

"Not my style."

Sutton smiled. "Noted."

She plated the food, the warm scent of citrus and fennel filling the space.

"This looks incredible," Wesley said.

“I cook when I’m stressed,” Sutton said.

She paused, then added with a smile, “Which is often. But not tonight.”

He lifted his glass in a half-toast.

“Cheers to coping mechanisms.”

Their glasses clinked softly.

As they ate, the conversation flowed more easily than she expected. Wesley recounted a tour mishap where the stage lights failed ten minutes into his first show, leaving him to perform three songs in near darkness.

“Did people buy it?” she asked, amusement bright in her eyes.

“Mostly. Except the one guy in the front row who yelled, ‘We want our money back!’ really killed the vibe.”

“Sounds like you recovered.”

“Maybe,” he said, modest grin tugging at his mouth. “Enough about me. Brynn mentioned you’re an event planner?”

Sutton paused mid-bite, caught off guard by the genuine curiosity in his voice.

“Yeah,” Sutton said, swirling her wine. “Mostly high-end galas and corporate things. Sometimes glamorous, other times not. The hours are long, especially around the holidays, but I love it. It keeps me on my toes.”

“Patience and creativity in spades, that’s impressive.”

He paused, then added,

“I can definitely relate to the ‘busy’ part.”

She arched an eyebrow.

"Your 'busy' probably looks way more glamorous than mine."

His smile softened, dimming around the edges.

"If you call living out of a suitcase and ordering room service at 2 a.m. glamorous."

He paused.

"It's not all it's cracked up to be."

A comfortable silence settled between them. Sutton caught the hint of weariness behind his words. It wasn't sadness but quiet exhaustion that he wore like a second skin.

She offered a small, understanding smile.

"You're still young. You've got time to figure it out."

He laughed low.

"Are you pulling the age card on me?"

"Maybe. But at least tonight came with homemade food."

"Tonight's already better," he said, and she felt the sincerity in it.

When they finished, Sutton began to gather dishes. Wesley stood quickly.

"Let me."

"You're the guest," she protested.

He plucked the towel from her hand, grinning.

"You cooked. I can handle cleanup."

She eyed him, amused.

"We can do it together."

They settled into it without thinking. Sutton washing, Wesley drying.

"I'll be honest," Wesley said quietly, wiping down the counter. "I missed this. It took a while after tour to feel normal again, without everything handled for me."

Sutton glanced at him.

"You poor little rich boy," she joked. "Normal's not so bad."

"No," he said softly, "it's not. Not bad at all."

Moonlight caught the angle of his profile as he turned toward the window.

"Thanks for letting me crash your quiet night."

Sutton smirked, lifting her glass.

"I didn't have much of a choice."

Wesley laughed, and they drank in easy silence, the kitchen soft and still. Nothing heavy, nothing charged, just the quiet beginning of something friendly.

Four

THE NEXT EVENING, THE group gathered at Northern Rail, a local bar with exposed brick, amber lights, and a storm-fueled crowd seeking refuge from the cold. Laughter drifted over the crowded chatter of conversation, the sound punctuated by clacks of pool balls and the ding of dartboards resetting.

Sutton leaned against a tall bar table, cocktail in hand, while Brynn perched beside her, eyes fixed on the pool table where Wesley lined up a shot with Marcus and Everett.

"So, tell me again," Brynn whispered, leaning in. "He walked in, saw you cooking, made small talk, and just happened to stay for dinner?"

"There's nothing to tell," Sutton said, rolling her eyes. "He came back for a jacket. I cooked. He stayed. It was a meal, not a date."

Brynn didn't even blink.

"Uh-huh."

Sutton avoided looking at her, taking a long sip of her drink.

"And you can't tell me you don't think he's cute," Brynn added, her voice singsong.

Sutton felt heat rise to her cheeks, but held her expression firm.

"He's twenty-five, Brynn."

"And you're thirty-three, not ninety."

Sutton crossed her arms.

"It's not the number. He still has so much life to live. And I'm not spending time with someone who's not even thinking about settling down."

Brynn sighed dramatically.

"You always make everything sound like a tax audit."

Sutton opened her mouth, but Brynn tilted her head toward Wesley, who was laughing with Marcus at the pool table, eyes bright under the warm light.

"Tell me you don't see it," Brynn murmured.

Sutton didn't answer. Which was still an answer.

A sudden clatter of balls broke through the noise as two young women approached Wesley, recognition lighting their faces.

"Excuse me, you're Wesley Preskott, right? Can we get a photo?"

Wesley straightened, offering a friendly smile.

"Of course."

Brynn shot Sutton a side-eye that said, "*Told you*" look.

Sutton shrugged it off, grabbed her empty glass, and turned to Cassie and Zoe.

"I'm getting another drink. Anyone want something?"

"I'll come," Zoe said, sliding off her stool.

At the bar, Sutton exhaled. She waved to the bartender for another round, then turned to Zoe.

"Seeing anyone these days?"

Zoe snorted.

"Not even close."

"Good," Sutton said with a grin. "Dating is exhausting."

"Tell me about it," Zoe replied, rolling her eyes fondly.

Sutton swirled her drink. "Anyone here catching your eye?"

Zoe laughed, not even pretending to be subtle, as her gaze drifted toward the pool table, specifically toward Wesley, who was lining up another shot.

Sutton followed her gaze, then shook her head with a knowing smile. It was obvious. Zoe was interested. Honestly, was everyone but her?

Zoe lifted her glass in a small salute.

"Cheers to whatever comes next."

Sutton felt warmth rise in her chest.

"Whatever comes next."

They headed back to the tables just as Marcus's voice boomed across the bar, louder than the jukebox.

"Look who's here!"

Sutton followed his gaze, and her breath hitched.

A tall figure shook snow from his coat near the entrance.

Brynn muttered, "Oh no."

"What's he doing here?" Sutton whispered, pulse quickening.

"I didn't know he was coming," Brynn said, eyes narrowing. "Swear."

Peter stepped forward. "Is that...?"

Brynn exhaled. "Yep. Graham."

The name landed like a stone in Sutton's stomach. Last winter's fling. Last winter's fireworks. Last winter's almost.

Graham scanned the bar and spotted her instantly. His smile spread, warm and familiar, confident without apology. He stopped at Marcus first, then met Wesley.

Then the group moved toward the bar tables, Graham's gaze flicking back to Sutton's surprised face.

"Hey, Sutton," he said, pulling her into a hug that lingered a beat too long.

She stepped back, her heart tripping.

"I didn't know you'd be here."

"Last-minute change," he said, eyes holding hers. "Didn't want to miss a chance to see everyone."

The air tightened. Conversations blurred into background static.

Sutton looked to Brynn, whose expression said everything her whisper didn't:

This is about to get complicated.

Five

THE MORNING AFTER THE whirlwind of the night before dawned slowly. A soft haze clung to the peaks around the tiny mountain town, sunlight stretching over the snow like spilled watercolor. The group scattered across the day, some tucked into cramped bookshops and quiet cafes, others strapped into their ski boots before Sutton had even risen.

Brynn and Marcus found each other as naturally as tides, slipping into their winter rhythm without effort. Their on-again fling resurfaced only during this trip each year, never more and never less. It wasn't complicated or secret, just a familiar comfort they stepped into when the snow fell. Sutton didn't bother defining it. Some bonds lived best in the in-between, untouched by labels or expectations.

By mid-afternoon, the group reconvened around a battered oak dining table in one of the town's lodges. The fireplace cracked and sighed, filling the air with the scent of melted butter, pine, and wood smoke. Bowls of stew and warm bread made their slow rotation around the table.

"Hey, are you done?"

Graham's voice cut through the low chatter.

Sutton looked up to find him standing at her shoulder, traces of cold clinging to his sweater. He looked exactly as she remembered: composed, handsome, and unmistakably himself.

She nodded and pushed her plate away.

"Sure."

His smile was brief but steady, a soft shift she felt in her ribs.

"Let's take a walk."

Heads at the table lifted. Brynn raised an eyebrow so high it nearly disappeared into her hairline. Sutton hesitated only a second; prolonging the tension would only make things worse.

Outside, the winter air kissed her cheeks, sharp and clean. Their boots crunched in unison across the fresh snow, mountains rising around them like silent guardians. Quiet settled over them.

"How have you been?" Sutton asked, her breath hanging in the cold.

Graham exhaled slowly, lifting his chin toward the horizon.

"Busy." He hesitated. "My grandmother passed last month."

His voice softened. "That was hard."

Sutton reached for his forearm, her fingers warm against wool.

"I'm really sorry. I know how much she meant to you."

He nodded once, absorbing the comfort without deflecting it. Then, after a beat:

"About last year, should we talk about it?"

Sutton's pulse stuttered, but she kept her voice even.

"There's nothing to talk about. We had a moment. It didn't become more, and that's okay."

He stopped walking and turned toward her fully. Snow groaned under his boots. His eyes held hers with unguarded clarity.

"We never talked about why," he said. "Last year was..."

"Special," she finished, giving him a small smile that felt both true and fragile.

Graham smiled.

"Timing is everything. It wasn't anyone's fault. We didn't make time for us after we left here."

She nodded, the truth sliding into place like a puzzle piece.

"We had something good," she said softly. "Maybe it was only meant to be a moment, not a forever."

He let out a quiet breath.

"Ever wonder what might've happened if we'd tried harder?"

"Sometimes," she admitted. "But if it was supposed to go further, it would have. We chose our own paths."

They fell into step again. The trail curved toward a wooden footbridge spanning a narrow creek, its surface glazed with ice. Light filtered through the evergreens, the world hushed and pale.

"It's beautiful here," Sutton murmured. Snowflakes clung to her hair like tiny crystals. "Romantic. Easy to get swept away."

Graham stepped a little closer, his sleeve brushing hers.

"Honestly? I came this week to see you. Not for some dramatic rekindling. Just to see if something still exists between us."

She stopped walking. The air felt thinner between them. He stood in front of her, confident, warm, more grounded than she remembered.

"There might always be something," he admitted, a wry smile tugging gently at his mouth. "But we never built a foundation. We never even tried to be friends before we rushed into everything else."

Sutton laughed, the memory bright against the cold air.

"That's very true."

"I'm glad I'm here now," he said.

Without thinking, she let her head rest lightly on his shoulder. The wool was coarse, but the warmth beneath it was familiar.

"Me too," she whispered.

Graham squeezed her hand once.

"Come on. Let's head back."

The walk returned in comfortable silence, snow crunching in rhythm as they retraced their path.

Back at the lodge, the dining room had emptied. Chairs sat pushed back, plates dusted with crumbs.

Graham turned to her with a grin.

"Dessert?"

She smiled. "My love language."

As he spoke to the hostess, she caught a glimpse of the corporate polish that still lingered. His sharp watch, the perfectly fitted sweater, softened now by something more human. It elicited the same feeling that had undone her before.

Six

THE LATE AFTERNOON LIGHT faded into evening as Wesley sat alone in Brynn's living room, fingers gliding lightly over the guitar strings. A soft, searching melody drifted into the room, mingling with the gentle crackle of the fireplace. The sound wasn't for an audience. It was for him. A quiet, unfiltered strum against the noise of the last year.

Even before he'd canceled the rest of his tour six months ago, the weight of detachment had crept in. His creativity had felt distant, as if he were perpetually on autopilot. But here, in this quiet cabin, he reconnected with the simplicity of playing for himself without the burden of expectation.

The front door clicked open. Sutton stepped inside, a rush of cold trailing in with her.

"Hey," she whispered. "Sorry, I didn't mean to interrupt."

Wesley smiled and set the guitar on the couch cushion beside him.

"No interruption. Just messing around."

She shrugged off her jacket, hanging it neatly by the door.

"Is Brynn around?"

"No," he said. "Pretty sure she's at Marcus's."

Sutton's lips curved knowingly.

"Of course she is."

Her laugh slipped easily into the room. Then she headed upstairs.

Wesley picked up the guitar again, letting his fingers fall back into a familiar progression.

When she reappeared, hair still damp, she crossed the room and opened the wine fridge.

"Did you want a glass?" she asked, already reaching for a bottle.

"Sure," Wesley said.

She poured two glasses, then hesitated.

"I don't want to interrupt your creative process. I can head upstairs if you need space."

Wesley shook his head.

"Not at all. I could use a break. And some company wouldn't hurt."

Sutton approached, her footsteps muffled against the hardwood.

"I feel like we need some Christmas music," she said, mischief dancing in her eyes before she began singing softly:

"Once bitten, twice shy. I keep my distance, but you still catch my eye..."

Wesley huffed out a laugh, surprise warming his expression. Instinctively, his fingers found the chords.

"Tell me, baby, do you recognize me?"

She climbed onto the couch beside him; the cushions dipped as their voices blurred into the chorus.

"Last Christmas, I gave you my heart."

Their laughter erupted as the last note faded, the sound bouncing off wooden walls.

"Hands down, one of my favorites," Sutton said, passing him a glass.

"It's a classic," he replied, leaning back.

The firelight cut warm strokes across her cheekbones, illuminating the curve of her smile.

The quiet stretched comfortably until Wesley asked, "So, how was your day with Graham?"

Sutton's fingers paused on her glass.

"It was fine. Nice to catch up. Town's pretty this time of year."

He nodded, sensing boundaries and choosing not to push them.

"What kind of music do you like?" he asked instead.

She gave him a look that was half amused, half accusing.

"Yours?"

"I don't mean mine," he protested, hands up, laughing.

Her laugh softened the moment.

“Everything. Country, pop, jazz, depends on the day. But Whitney’s ‘I Wanna Dance With Somebody’, that’s a forever favorite.”

Inspiration flickered in his eyes. His hands returned to the guitar, coaxing an intimate, slow-burning version of the opening chords. Sutton’s eyes fluttered shut, her body swaying gently.

When she opened them again, her inhale slipped away.

“Your voice,” she whispered, goosebumps rising along her arms.

“That was unreal.”

Her sincerity landed deeper than any arena roar.

Wesley began playing again, a softer melody now, introspective and warm. Sutton leaned back into the cushions, watching his fingers move.

“How can you ever leave music?” she murmured. “It’s so clearly a part of who you are.”

He looked up, surprised by the tenderness in her voice.

“I can’t,” he said quietly. “I just sometimes forget why I started.”

She nodded and kept listening.

“It’s been a hard year,” Wesley said, staring into his wine. “The pressure, the constant movement. I didn’t realize how far I’d drifted from myself until I finally stopped.”

He let out a slow breath, fingers brushing absently over the calluses on his fingertips.

“Music has always been my life. It’s a map of experiences. It connects people to moments, places, memories. That’s what

I love about it." He paused. "But being the musician is exhausting."

His gaze dropped again.

"And then I went through a breakup," he said quietly. "Which always feels like a recalibration. Learning how to be one person again instead of part of something shared."

Sutton thought of the headlines, two musicians trying to make room for each other until they couldn't.

Her hand reached out, fingers brushing his arm.

"I'm sorry. Breakups are hard enough without everything else piling on."

He met her eyes.

"Being here helps. Talking without an agenda. It's been a while since I had that."

"Sometimes," Sutton said, voice low, "stepping back is the only way forward."

He studied her for a moment.

"What about you? Are you happy?"

"I went through a phase in my late twenties where I had to step back and figure out who I was outside everyone else's expectations," she said. "What matters to me now are moments like this."

She gestured between them, the movement sending a small ripple through her glass.

Wesley took that in.

"It took a lot of vulnerability, and a lot of accepting my flaws, but I came out the other side with a true understanding of who I am, what I value, and what matters."

Her voice carried no pretense, just quiet certainty.

"I honestly believe that finding your way out of the darkness takes time and support," Sutton added, her words barely louder than the fire's whisper. "It's challenging, and it varies from person to person, but for me, focusing on self-reflection brought about a significant change."

Wesley studied her, the shadows playing across her face.

"It's rare to meet someone who knows themselves that well," he said, the words coming out rougher than intended.

Sutton's smile deepened, crinkling at the corners.

"Maybe you're going through what I did," she said quietly. "Different circumstances, obviously."

"Maybe," Wesley said, lifting his glass.

She hesitated, then added, almost lightly, "Sometimes I forget you're only twenty-five."

He smiled, unfazed.

"Is that a compliment, or a warning?"

She laughed under her breath.

"It's just that you don't *act* like most guys your age."

His shoulders lifted in a small shrug.

"Most twenty-five-year-olds haven't had the same responsibilities I've had."

Her smile faded, thought overtaking it.

"It's not really the number. It's where people are."

He tilted his head.

"Shared values matter more than matching timelines."

She didn't argue. The quiet stretched between them.

He went back to playing, but the song had changed. Softer now. More careful.

Sutton drifted closer without thinking, settling into the quiet of it, into how natural it felt to sit here with him.

When Wesley's hands finally stilled on the guitar, the silence that followed wasn't empty. It held something neither of them had meant to invite.

Sutton inhaled slowly, steadying herself.

"I should get some sleep. It's late."

Wesley nodded once.

"Yeah. Of course. Goodnight, Sutton."

She stood. Each step toward the stairs took effort, as though leaving required more intention than staying.

Seven

THE MORNING BROKE CRISP and clear, the cold that felt clean in the lungs. Perfect for the group's annual winter games.

What had started years ago as a spontaneous snowball fight had evolved into a full winter sports day, a cherished tradition now. Brynn, always determined to outdo herself, had organized a lineup of events: a snowman-building showdown, a relay race in ridiculous oversized gear, and an ice-sculpting contest complete with kits she'd ordered online at two in the morning.

Everyone buzzed with anticipation, bundled in puffy jackets and mismatched hats. Marcus passed out bright green and blue scarves to divide them into teams, his grin full of mischief.

"Remember when there were only seven of us dumb enough to do this?" he said.

Laughter rippled through the group.

"Please," Cassie added, "Peter fell face-first into his own snowman the first year."

“I was testing structural integrity,” Peter shot back, already smirking before the laughter hit again.

“Alright!” Brynn called out. “Green team, blue team, take your places! Snowman challenge first!”

Sutton tied her blue scarf and glanced around. Her teammates were Wesley and Zoe.

Across the snowy lawn, Graham, a green scarf wrapped around his neck, caught her eye and shot her a playful grin.

“Ready to lose gracefully?” he teased.

“Not a chance,” Sutton said, gesturing at Wesley. “We’ve got our secret weapon.”

Wesley blinked at her.

“I didn’t know I was a weapon, but sure.”

The whistle blew, and chaos erupted.

Snow flew in every direction, shouts filling the crisp air. Wesley crouched down immediately, packing snow with professional concentration.

“We need a sturdy base,” he said, already molding the foundation. “Dense, or it’ll collapse.”

Sutton rolled a snowball bigger than she expected, breath fogging the air.

Zoe sprinted toward the tree line.

“I’ll get decorations! Someone find me a carrot before Marcus does!”

Across the field, Graham’s team was already unraveling. Marcus hoisted an absurdly large middle section.

“It’s too big!”

"Go big or go home!" Graham insisted, absolutely committed to architectural disaster.

Wesley smoothed the snowman's body with careful precision.

"Zoe! Head status?"

"Head secured!" she announced proudly, carrying a perfect snowball.

Sutton pressed the carrot into place. Pebble eyes. Stick arms. A scarf tied neatly around the neck.

Wesley stepped back, cheeks pink from the cold.

"Okay, we crushed this."

Brynn's whistle pierced the air.

"Time's up!"

The blue team's snowman stood tall and symmetrical, practically glowing in the winter light.

The green team's snowman leaned. Dramatically.

Its head was so oversized it appeared to be contemplating an escape.

Marcus circled their snowman with faux seriousness.

"An avant-garde interpretation of balance."

Everett squinted at the green team's creation.

"Looks like it survived an avalanche."

After unnecessary deliberation and whispered theatrics, Brynn threw both hands up.

"Next event: relay race!"

The relay race required each team member to don enormous boots, giant mittens, and an oversized parka before bolting down a snowy obstacle course.

"On your marks... get set... GO!"

Wesley went first. The boots flopped wildly, his arms windmilling for balance as he waddled over snow hurdles.

"Run like a penguin!" Zoe shrieked, doubled over laughing.

Wesley grabbed a puzzle piece and lumbered back, breathless and triumphant.

Zoe jammed her feet into the giant boots and immediately toppled backward into the snow.

"I feel like a marshmallow with legs!"

Sutton hauled her up, laughing.

"Come on, Marshmallow. We've got a puzzle to finish."

Zoe completed her leg of the race, and then Sutton took off for her "run", which was more of an enthusiastic waddle. She hurdled the snow piles, arms flailing and laughter bubbling from her chest.

Further down the course, Graham tripped, landing face-first in a drift.

"You good?" Sutton called.

He popped up with snow in his hair.

"Never better."

They finished breathless and cheering. Brynn clapped wildly.

"Last event, ice sculpting!"

At the ice blocks, Brynn handed out chisels like a proud game-show host.

"Forty-five minutes! Go create!"

Wesley stared seriously at his block.

"We need a plan."

"Rabbit," Zoe declared immediately.

Wesley blinked.

"Rabbit. Sure. Why not?"

Sutton crouched beside him, breath visible in the cold.

"Can you make a rabbit?"

"Guess we'll find out," he murmured.

He worked carefully, shaping the snow bit by bit. Long ears took form, then a rounded head, small paws.

Sutton watched in quiet admiration.

"Maybe you missed your calling," she teased.

Wesley glanced at their progress.

"There's still time for a career change."

Across the way, Graham was attacking his ice block.

"Abstract art!" he announced, chips flying everywhere. "This is going to revolutionize the world."

Marcus squinted.

"It looks like it's screaming."

Brynn's whistle eventually ended the chaos.

The blue team's rabbit was charming, delicate, and recognizable.

The green team's sculpture resembled an iceberg fleeing the Titanic.

"Chaos in Winter!" Graham declared proudly.

The group roared with laughter.

By nightfall, the group had gathered around a blazing bonfire, its flames snapping upward as if trying to warm the falling dusk. The scent of wood smoke curled through the clearing. Marshmallow blistered over open flames and laughter drifted into the chilly mountain air like soft sparks.

Brynn stood, cheeks flushed with triumph as she tallied the final scores with theatrical flair.

"And the winner of this year's winter games is..."

She paused dramatically, drawing out the silence until everyone leaned in.

"...the blue team!"

Sutton, Wesley, and Zoe shot to their feet, erupting with delighted cheers.

Across the circle, Graham lifted his mug toward Sutton in a small salute.

"Well played," he called, the words carrying easily across the firelight.

Beside her, Zoe nudged Wesley with her elbow.

"I'm pretty sure my snowman artistry clinched it," she bragged, grinning.

"Team effort," Wesley said, amusement tipping his voice. His glance drifted briefly across the fire toward Sutton, a flicker small but unmistakably drawn.

Zoe caught it.

She didn't stiffen or retreat. Instead, she accepted the marshmallow stick he passed her; her smile gentle instead of jealous.

"It was fun," she said quietly, the firelight softening her features. "I haven't laughed like this in ages."

"Me neither," Wesley admitted, the confession slipping out before he could temper it.

Her voice dipped, touched with something light but intentional.

"Maybe we should find more excuses for fun."

Wesley chuckled, warm but careful.

"Not a bad idea."

Zoe winked as she turned her marshmallow over the flame.

"Then just remember who you want on your team next time."

Across the fire, Sutton and Graham stood at the makeshift bar, close enough that their conversation stayed between them. Familiar, low.

When Graham reached for a bottle, his hand brushed the small of Sutton's back. Light. Confident. It stayed there a beat longer than necessary.

Sutton didn't step away.

The moment struck Wesley like a cold draft. Not jealousy, not the sharp kind he'd always imagined. Something quieter. Bruising. A tightening he hadn't expected.

Beside him, Brynn noticed. She always did.

Her gaze followed his for a moment, then returned to him.

"Old flames," she said lightly, though her eyes held more weight. "Never simple."

Wesley's jaw flexed before he spoke.

"There's a lot of history here," he murmured, as if the admission alone required effort.

Brynn bumped her shoulder gently against his.

"Good material for a song?" she teased.

He tried to laugh, but it came out quiet, thin around the edges.

A log cracked in the fire, sending a swirl of sparks into the air. Snow began to fall, soft and powdery, dusting the edges of boots and blankets and the tops of wine bottles.

Brynn leaned in closer, her voice dropping to something only he could hear.

"Just remember," she murmured, "some stories aren't meant to be watched from the sidelines."

Snow continued to fall.

The fire burned on.

Eight

One Year Ago

The trattoria glowed with a warmth that made everything seem a little softer, a little easier to feel. Candlelight flickered off ruby-colored wine, shadows danced across terra-cotta walls, and the air swirled with the intoxicating mix of tomato, garlic, and basil simmering somewhere in the back.

Sutton felt the moment shift before it happened.

Graham reached across the crisp white linen tablecloth, his fingertips brushing hers.

"Sutton," he said, setting down his fork with a quiet clink that felt louder than it should have. "I should probably tell you. I'm not good at casual."

A smile tugged at her lips, unbidden and softer than she meant it to be. She glanced down at her hands, faint traces of flour from the afternoon's gnocchi lesson still clinging to her fingers.

She'd never been good at pretending things didn't matter.

"Not good at casual," she repeated, letting the words settle. "Well. That makes two of us."

He laughed, the sound easy across the table. Graham didn't crowd her or rush; he just watched her, patient, giving her space to speak if she wanted to.

Dinner slipped by in shared plates and unguarded laughter, the kind that lingered longer than intended.

When they stepped out into the winter night, the air was crisp enough to steal her breath. Snow fell lightly, catching the yellow glow of the streetlamps and softening the quiet road.

Graham slid an arm around her waist, pulling her closer as they walked. The warmth pressed through her coat, steady and sure. She let herself lean into it.

When they reached Brynn's cabin, he stopped at the bottom of the stairs and turned her toward him. The porch light caught his face, sharpening the calm certainty there without softening it.

"I've been wanting to do this all night," he murmured, his thumb tracing a gentle line along her jaw—confident, but never careless.

Her pulse jumped.

He took a breath.

"Tonight mattered to me," he said. "I don't want to overthink it. I just know I want more of this. More of you."

Inside, the door barely clicked shut before their coats fell to the floor. The shift from cold to warmth felt disorienting, like stepping back into something she hadn't touched in a long time.

Graham reached for her, his hands settling at the small of her back. He kissed her shoulder first, then the curve of her neck, then higher, until she turned into him completely.

Their lips met with a heat that surprised her, not because it was bold, but because she met it without hesitation.

There were no mixed signals. No guessing.

With Graham, things were clear.

He seemed to know when to slow, when to draw her closer. She responded before she could think, following instinct where logic had already stepped aside.

By the end of the night, it was impossible to pretend nothing had begun.

Something had started.

It mattered, even if it didn't stay.

NINE

PRESENT DAY

SUTTON LAY AWAKE IN the soft hush of her bedroom, moonlight pooling across the sheets in pale bands. The city was quiet for once, the kind of quiet that left too much room for thought.

Inevitably, her mind drifted back to last winter's trip.

To Graham.

That night had settled into her memory easily, almost too easily. The trattoria's candlelight, the blur of snow beyond the window, the weight of his hand over hers on the white linen tablecloth. His gaze had been steady, attentive, the kind that made her lower her guard without realizing she had.

She had been swept up.

At the time, it had felt simple. Well-timed.

Then life had rushed back in, and whatever they were during the trip had been overtaken by everything waiting on the other side of it.

Now the memory lingered, present but contained. When his hand brushed her lower back earlier, it carried the same familiarity. Comforting. Predictable. A feeling tied to who they had been then, not necessarily who they were now.

She pulled the blanket higher, her breath slow.

Had anything truly shifted between them?

Or was she holding onto a moment that had already passed?

***

The next morning, sunlight poured through the café's tall windows, catching on mismatched velvet chairs and the gilded edges of antique mirrors. The air smelled of espresso and cinnamon. It felt like a place where people leaned in and said things out loud, and Brynn treated it as such.

"Alright," Brynn declared, leaning forward like a detective on a case. "Spill. Everything."

Sutton blinked.

"You don't even say hello first?"

"There's no time for hello." Brynn waved her off. "Graham. Wesley. Start talking."

Sutton laughed into her coffee.

"It's complicated."

Brynn's eyes gleamed.

"My favorite flavor."

Sutton swirled her cup, watching the ripples settle.

"Seeing Graham yesterday stirred up more than I expected. Last winter feels like a movie I rented and never returned."

"A very steamy movie," Brynn corrected.

Sutton gave her a look.

"It felt magical. But after the trip, neither of us fought for it. Life got busy. We let it fade."

Brynn folded her arms, skeptical.

"Has he changed?"

"That's what I'm trying to figure out." Sutton rested her elbows on the table. "He's charming, successful, thoughtful. On paper, we make sense. But on paper doesn't build anything. And effort was never really his thing."

"So the Graham of yesterday might still be the Graham of today," Brynn said.

Sutton's smile was small but knowing.

"Pretty much."

Brynn took a slow sip of her latte.

"Still hot, though."

Sutton snorted.

"Painfully."

"So you're tempted?" Brynn pressed.

"I'm curious," Sutton said. "But not convinced."

Brynn nodded once.

"Okay. Fair. But now we need to talk about Wesley."

Sutton tipped her head back.

"Oh, my God."

"Oh yes, we're going there." Brynn pointed at her. "I've seen the way you two look at each other."

"He's different," Sutton said slowly. "Fun. Easy to talk to. But Brynn, he's twenty-five. I'm thirty-three. He's famous. I'm not."

"Age and fame," Brynn dismissed with a dramatic swipe of her hand. "Please. Chemistry doesn't care about resumes."

Sutton hesitated.

"It also doesn't handle tour buses, fangirls, and a global stage."

"Oh, is that what's holding you back?" Brynn teased. "Or is it the girls begging for selfies?"

Sutton shook her head, laughing.

"Possibly both."

Brynn leaned in, chin in hand.

"Look, I'm not saying marry either of them. But the way you talk about Wesley..."

She paused.

"You light up a little."

Sutton's cheeks warmed.

"We're just getting to know each other."

"You're wading," Brynn said, wiggling her eyebrows. "Into the shallow end of his pool."

"Please stop with the metaphors."

"No. I refuse." Brynn grinned. "Eventually you'll be floating with sunglasses and a cocktail in someone's pool."

Sutton laughed.

"You're ridiculous."

"Maybe," Brynn said. "But also correct."

Her voice softened.

"In all seriousness, I'm glad you're letting yourself feel something again. Graham or Wesley, whoever. You deserve good things, Sutton."

Sutton's smile gentled.

"Thanks. It feels messy. But maybe a good mess."

Brynn raised her cup.

"To excitement."

Sutton tapped hers against it.

"And cannonballs in the pool when the time is right."

They clinked, the sound bright against the low morning hum of the café.

Ten

The group wound through the narrow streets of the nearby town, their laughter rising in pale bursts as they stepped into a bustling restaurant glowing with candlelight. Warmth met them immediately. Voices layered over clinking glassware. The scent of grilled meat and simmering spices filled the room.

At the long wooden table, coats were draped over chair backs, drinks beaded with condensation beside flickering candles, conversations overlapping with easy familiarity. Sutton settled into the seat beside Graham, their shoulders brushing whenever they leaned in to hear each other over the hum of the room.

His presence was familiar. Assured. Threaded with history. It tugged at her more than she wanted to acknowledge. Each casual touch carried an echo of last winter, stirring something she'd told herself had cooled.

Across the table, Wesley noticed.

It wasn't just the way Graham angled toward her or the softness in her replies. It was the glances she sent across the table, quick and unguarded, that landed on Wesley before she looked away. Too brief to mean nothing. Too frequent to be accidental.

Beside him, Zoe leaned closer, her hand brushing his forearm.

"You've been quiet tonight," she said, her voice gentle.

Wesley offered a polite smile.

"Just taking it all in."

"Mm-hm." Zoe narrowed her eyes, amused. "I work in a hospital. Reading people is basically my entire day."

He let out a small laugh.

"You've got something going on in there," she added, tapping lightly at her temple. "More than you want to say."

Wesley didn't deny it. He lifted only a shoulder.

"Maybe."

Zoe's tone softened.

"I just got out of a two-year thing. I know the look. Sometimes the trick is to stop trying to make sense of everything."

He considered that.

"Being in the moment."

"Exactly." Zoe smiled. "Let things be what they are."

Before he could answer, Marcus shot up from his chair and pointed at Brynn with theatrical horror.

"Brynn only loves Eagle Ridge because the lodge serves that ridiculous hot chocolate. Deny it."

Brynn gasped, pressing a hand to her chest.

"Ridiculous? It's a masterpiece. Also, better snow, a better lodge, and the bartender is extremely easy on the eyes."

Zoe groaned.

"Oh, please. London boys are a drag."

Brynn winked.

"You know I love me a London boy."

The table erupted. Even Sutton laughed, something in her chest easing for the first time that night.

Graham leaned in then, his breath warm against her ear.

"You seem distracted."

She exhaled. "Just a lot on my mind."

His fingers brushed her arm.

"If you ever want to talk."

Sutton smiled, brief and grateful.

"I know."

Across the table, Marcus leaned toward Brynn, not nearly quiet enough.

"Looks like we've got another winter couple forming."

Brynn's eyes narrowed.

"Marcus. Do not start."

Too late. The words lingered, brittle in the space between them.

Wesley heard.

He didn't react, not outwardly. He lifted his whiskey and took a slow sip, his shoulders drawing in a fraction as he retreated to somewhere guarded.

Brynn caught it. She straightened and raised her glass.

"To new adventures, old friends, and whatever chaos tomorrow brings."

Glasses lifted. Laughter followed.

The moment smoothed itself over, at least on the surface.

As dinner wound down. Graham leaned toward Sutton again, his voice low.

"Come on. Let's grab a nightcap across the street."

The invitation was easy. Familiar. His expression held an expectation she recognized, one that pulled at her even as it gave her pause.

For a moment, she almost said yes.

But something tugged back. Something quieter. Something new.

"I think I'm going to head to the cabin," she said gently. "I'm wiped."

Disappointment crossed his face before he smoothed it away.

"Another time."

Outside, cold air wrapped around them in a sharp sweep. Sutton tugged her coat tighter, already imagining the quiet cabin waiting for her. Brynn fell into step alongside her, voice dipped low.

"Just so you know," Brynn said, a hint of mischief there, "I'm staying at Marcus's tonight. Cabin's yours."

The implication landed before Sutton had time to sort through it.

Her pulse stuttered.

Her gaze drifted, almost involuntarily, to Wesley a few steps away, adjusting his scarf. His breath clouded in the air. When he glanced up and caught her looking, he didn't smile, just held her gaze for a beat longer than necessary.

The drive back to the cabin settled into a low, steady quiet. Wesley sat angled toward the window, watching the lights streak past, his thoughts elsewhere. Every so often he glanced her way, quick and uncertain, as if he wasn't sure he should linger.

Sutton felt each look all the same.

Then, without warning, he straightened and pointed at a bright sign flashing along the roadside.

WORLD'S BEST PIE — OPEN LATE.

"That," he said with a sudden grin, "is something I can never resist on tour."

There was a lightness in his voice she hadn't heard all night.

Sutton let out a soft laugh.

"World's best? Pretty bold claim."

Only a beat passed before she flicked on her blinker.

"Well. There's only one way to find out."

Wesley's grin turned boyish and unguarded.

"This is already the highlight of my night."

He unbuckled as she parked, stepping into the cold as if shedding whatever had been weighing on him. Sutton rounded the hood of the car and shot him a teasing look.

"If this pie is terrible, you're banned from future roadside recommendations."

“Fair enough.” He held the diner door open for her. “But I’ve got faith in this place.”

He nodded toward the glowing display case.

“I mean. It’s pie.”

Sutton laughed as she stepped inside.

For a moment, under the bright diner lights with the cold sealed off behind them, it felt like they’d slipped into something simple and unexpected. Not a beginning she could define yet, but one she didn’t rush to step away from.

ELEVEN

SUTTON HADN'T MEANT FOR the night to stretch beyond dinner, yet here she was, tucked into a retro diner booth across from Wesley, sharing pie under neon lights that flickered like something out of a forgotten movie.

The place felt suspended in time. Black-and-white checkered floors, chrome trim, the low hum of an old jukebox softening the edges of the evening. The scent of cinnamon and sugar lingered in the air, warm and familiar.

She ordered key lime. He chose apple, still hot enough that steam rose when he cut into it.

But it wasn't the pie that surprised her.

It was how easy everything felt.

Their conversation drifted from childhood embarrassments to favorite films to the concerts that had changed them. Laughter came without effort, punctuated by the occasional brush of knees beneath the table. Each story Wesley shared revealed something slightly unexpected. Fame had reshaped parts of him, sharpening some edges, leaving others exposed.

For Wesley, sitting across from Sutton felt like finally letting out a breath. She wasn't reaching for the persona or the polish. She was simply there, meeting him where he was.

He hadn't realized how much he'd been missing that.

They were halfway through their slices when a young woman approached, her hands trembling around her phone.

"Are you Wesley Preskott?" she asked, her voice thin with nerves.

Sutton leaned back slightly, giving them space. The intimacy of the evening bent, but it didn't break.

Wesley's smile was kind and practiced. Sutton caught the flicker beneath it. Weariness. Acceptance. A weight he carried without comment.

He posed for a quick photo, signed her napkin, then slid back into the booth with a slow exhale.

"Sorry," he murmured. "That happens less these days, but when it does..."

He lifted one shoulder, the gesture small.

"It must feel strange," Sutton said, keeping her voice low, "to be so accessible to strangers."

"Strange is the perfect word." He let out a short laugh that didn't quite reach his eyes.

He hesitated, then met her gaze more directly.

"Most people want something. A picture. Proof." He paused. "But you don't."

He stopped himself, a faint smile forming.

"You don't treat me like that."

"Like what?" she asked.

"Like I'm a headline."

Sutton didn't rush her answer.

"Well," she said, "you're not."

Her smile was simple.

"You're a person. And I like getting to know that person."

His smile, when it came, was small and genuine.

"Me too."

***

The drive back to Brynn's cabin settled into a quiet warmth. The radio hummed low, headlights cutting through drifting snow. When Sutton pulled into the driveway, the porch light washed the cabin in gold, the moment suddenly private.

Inside, she shrugged out of her jacket, moving with the unhurried ease of someone not quite ready for the night to end. Wesley followed her in. The door clicked shut behind them, sealing off the cold.

She turned toward the staircase. Sleep tugged at her, but something else tugged harder.

At the base of the steps, her hand brushed his arm. Light. Fleeting.

Not accidental.

Wesley stilled.

His fingers closed gently around her forearm, the touch a question rather than an assumption. The air shifted, thinning and thickening all at once. Sutton turned toward him, the space between them narrowing.

"You make things feel lighter," he said quietly.

Her breath slipped out before she could stop it. He noticed.

"And you make everything feel real," she said.

Something in him settled, subtle but decisive. He stepped closer. Slowly, carefully, he reached up and tucked a loose strand of hair behind her ear. His fingers brushed her jaw, and her composure loosened, piece by piece.

"Sutton," he said, her name soft, unfinished.

She didn't move away.

He leaned in, not rushing, not assuming. She met him halfway, her chin lifting, eyes closing.

The kiss was gentle at first, exploratory. When it deepened, it stayed deliberate, unhurried. A question asked and answered at once.

Her hand found the sleeve of his jacket, holding there. His settled at the back of her neck, steadying.

When they finally pulled apart, their foreheads hovered close, breaths mingling in the quiet.

"Goodnight, Sutton," he said, his voice slightly off balance.

"Goodnight."

He lingered a moment, then turned and took the stairs. She watched until he disappeared from view.

Only then did Sutton lift her fingers to her lips, her heart beating faster than she expected.

Upstairs, behind a closed door, Wesley leaned back against the wood, breath uneven.

The kiss complicated everything.

But one truth remained.

He didn't regret it.

Twelve

On the seventh morning of the winter retreat, the living room of Marcus's cabin looked like the interior of a glossy holiday catalog. Pine garlands draped across doorways, twinkling lights reflected in every window, ribbons of crimson and gold catching firelight as people passed through.

Zoe stood in the center, her phone in hand, scrolling through their ever-growing checklist.

"Alright," she said, tapping the screen. "We're two days out. Are we solid?"

"Mostly," Marcus replied, surveying the room with theatrical pride. "Menu's done. Décor's getting there. Honestly, it's giving 'holiday royalty'."

He turned to Brynn.

"Caterer confirmed?"

Brynn nodded, practically vibrating with excitement.

"Yep. Last call is tomorrow morning. They're ready."

The holiday dinner, set for Day Nine, had become the heart of the trip. A night to dress up, exchange small gifts, and toast another year of friendships that had stretched across cities, jobs, breakups, and everything in between. Less a tradition now than a promise.

"I swear, this is my favorite part of the entire trip," Sutton said as she smoothed a velvet table runner. "It's like Christmas morning at night."

Marcus slung an arm around Brynn, surveying the sparkling room.

"Epic, as always."

Brynn nudged him.

"We do throw the best holiday party."

"You mean I do."

"You wish."

Their bickering rose like smoke.

But for Sutton, the cheerful chaos pressed in. Too many voices. Too many undercurrents she wasn't ready to examine. She slipped away quietly, bundling into her scarf before stepping out into the cold.

The small mountain town was wrapped in winter charm. Shop windows glowed with warm light; wreaths hung on every door. Snow crunched beneath Sutton's boots as she wandered through stores, letting her fingers skim handmade ornaments and wool scarves.

She needed quiet.

She needed space to breathe, to let her thoughts settle.

Graham.

Wesley.

Two names. Two gravitational pulls. Two completely different versions of possibility.

***

Across town, laughter skimmed over the wind at the ice rink. Peter, Cassie, Graham, and Wesley had joined the swirl of locals and families skating beneath strings of lights.

"Stand back," Peter announced as he stepped onto the ice with the confidence of someone who had absolutely none.

Seconds later, he wiped out spectacularly, clinging to Cassie with a strangled yelp.

Cassie steadied him, laughing so hard she nearly fell too.

"You fall with style," she said, breathless.

Graham and Wesley glided past them effortlessly. Wesley's movements were smooth, surprisingly graceful, more dancer than rockstar. Graham, of course, refused to be shown up.

"Think you can keep up?" Wesley teased.

Graham grinned, competitive to his core.

"Watch me."

They pushed into the race, their laughter ringing across the rink. Their breaths formed twin trails of mist in the cold air.

After a few rounds, they drifted to the edge, unlacing skates with numb fingers.

Graham rubbed his palms together.

“So, first time on this winter trip?”

“Yeah,” Wesley said. “First time. Kind of loving the break from everything.”

Graham nodded.

“It’s like stepping out of your own life for a minute. Glad I came back this year.”

Their silence mingled with the steady scrape of blades on ice. Children shrieked, couples kissed under mistletoe decorations, and teenagers skated hand-in-hand.

Graham broke the silence.

“So, when you’re not touring the world, what do you do for fun?”

“Honestly? Music is fun,” Wesley said. “But lately I’ve gotten into photography. Something creative without pressure.”

“Good outlet,” Graham said. “Keeps you sane.”

Wesley nodded, and for a moment, the camaraderie felt easy.

Too easy.

He liked Graham.

He understood Graham.

And that made everything more complicated.

Graham’s gaze drifted back toward the ice, a thoughtful shadow crossing his expression.

“I’ve noticed you and Sutton seem close,” he said, his voice careful.

Wesley kept his tone neutral.

“I wouldn’t say close. She’s just easy to talk to.”

Graham let out a slow breath.

"Last year, she and I spent a lot of time together. It was intense. Brief." A quiet honesty softened his voice. "When we got back to New York, work swallowed me alive. I didn't make enough space for us."

Wesley didn't interrupt.

The admission threaded something unfamiliar through his chest.

"She's not someone you let go of easily," Graham said.

The words settled between them.

Wesley kept his voice low, nearly lost beneath the rink's music.

"Do you think there's a chance the two of you might try again?"

Graham's jaw tightened.

"I don't know." He paused. "I'd like to think there's something left. But I guess we'll see."

The rink surged back into focus, laughter and blades cutting the ice. None of it touched the quiet forming between them.

Wesley swallowed.

"She seems like someone worth the effort."

Graham nodded, the look on his face almost wistful.

"She is."

Wesley turned back to the spinning lights overhead, the knot in his chest tightening. For the first time, he wondered if Sutton's heart might already be drifting somewhere he couldn't follow.

Thirteen

After her reflective walk downtown, Sutton returned to the cabin feeling steadier than she had all afternoon. Voices carried from the living room, threaded with laughter.

The moment she stepped inside, Wesley's gaze found hers. Instinctive. Immediate. The quiet brightness in his eyes caught her off guard. Before she could unbutton her scarf, he rose from the sofa and followed her into the kitchen, peeling away from the group until the rest of the room faded.

"Hey," he said softly. "How was your walk?"

"It was nice." Sutton smiled, still carrying the calm she'd found in town. "This place is magical at Christmas. Even the lampposts look like they're trying too hard."

His mouth curved, something deeper flickering beneath the humor.

"Good. The rink was fun too. Graham is more competitive than I expected."

Sutton laughed.

"Yes, he is. It's one thing I like about him. He's always up for a challenge."

Something crossed Wesley's expression, quick and contained. He rested a hand against the counter, fingers brushing the edge.

"We talked a bit after skating," he said, his voice lower. "He mentioned last year. The two of you."

Sutton stilled, her hand closing around a water bottle.

"Oh?" she said lightly. "He did?"

Wesley nodded once, exhaling slowly.

"I don't want to step into anything messy. Last night..."

"You didn't," she said quickly, sharper than she meant. She softened.

"You didn't," she repeated, quieter.

They stood suspended in that thin space between meaning and restraint.

Until Zoe appeared in the doorway like a burst of champagne fizz.

"Where's the wine opener?" she asked, waving a bottle.

Sutton blinked, stepped aside, and grabbed it.

"Right here."

She nudged Zoe back toward the living room, slipping easily into cheer. Before leaving, she cast one last look at Wesley, half apology, half unfinished sentence.

Then she disappeared.

The moment fractured.

Later, the cabin filled with the scent of grilled food and wood smoke. Everyone crowded around the fire, laughter bouncing off logs and beams, but Wesley felt oddly unmoored, like he'd left part of himself standing in that kitchen.

Zoe lingered near him, her smile warm, her hand brushing his arm with deliberate softness. She was lovely, attentive, easy to talk to. None of it quieted the restless twist in his chest.

His attention kept drifting toward the window.

Outside, Sutton and Brynn stood by the fire pit, their silhouettes etched in flickering gold. Then Graham joined them. Something tightened low in Wesley's stomach, an ache he couldn't justify but couldn't ignore.

Brynn drifted away, leaving Sutton and Graham alone with the flames.

Wesley couldn't hear their words, but he could feel the history. The way Graham angled toward her. Sutton didn't step away.

That softness.

That familiarity.

Inside, his bottle warmed in his hand. Outside, the air crackled.

Sutton kept her gaze on the fire as Graham approached.

"Beautiful night, isn't it?" he said, eyes lifting briefly to the stars before settling on her.

"It is," she replied, though distance threaded her voice.

Graham inhaled as if steadying himself.

"I'm just going to say it. What we had last year mattered to me. I let it slip. Work took over, and I didn't show up the way I should have."

Sutton's chest tightened.

"I'm in a different place now," he continued. "Let me take you out after the trip. A real date. Just us. See if there's still something there."

His smile was the same one that had undone her last winter. For a second, memory tugged.

But it didn't move her the way it once had.

"I don't know, Graham," she said. "Last year was beautiful. But when we got back to the city, it didn't last. And that hurt."

Regret shifted his features.

"I know. And I'm sorry. But give me a chance to show you it can be different."

The words hovered. Warm. Hopeful. Heavy.

But her thoughts were already drifting toward a different shape.

Wesley.

Sutton's breath caught when she spotted him inside the cabin near the window. She watched him set his bottle on the counter and turn away.

Graham's voice pulled her back.

"So," he said carefully. "What do you think?"

She glanced once more toward the window, then back at him.

"I need some time," she said, already closing the conversation.

He nodded, disappointment flickering before he masked it.

"I understand."

She stepped away, then paused. The moment deserved that much.

"I promise," she said, a polite smile lifting her mouth. "I'll think about it."

Then she slipped through the side gate toward the front of the cabin, following fresh footprints away from the firelight and into the cold.

"Wesley," she called, breath visible as she hurried across the snow. "Where are you going?"

He stopped, shoulders softening.

"Just needed some air," he said, offering a tired smile that didn't quite reach his eyes.

She closed the distance.

"Mind if I join you? We never finished our conversation."

He nodded, and they fell into step together.

"Last night," he said after a moment. "I didn't plan it. It just happened."

His gaze met hers.

"And I don't regret it."

Her pulse fluttered.

"Me neither."

"But it complicates things," she said. "You're young. You're famous. The world wants a piece of you. And we're in this snow-globe bubble." She gestured to the street. "I've been here before."

Wesley stepped closer.

"I know."

He hesitated.

"So you and Graham?"

"He wants to try again. After the trip. A real shot."

"And do you want that?"

She swallowed.

"I thought maybe I did. Then you kissed me, and everything I'd been pushing away felt alive again."

Relief softened his face.

"I feel it too."

He moved closer, slow and deliberate.

"That kiss felt right to me," he said gently. "Still does."

Her breath hitched.

"Me too."

He leaned in. When their lips met, the world quieted. The kiss was soft but certain, warm against the cold night, unhurried even as her heart raced. Her fingers curled into his coat. His hand settled at the back of her neck, steady and reverent.

When they parted, their foreheads stayed close.

"We're in a bubble," she whispered. "This isn't the real world."

"Maybe," Wesley said, his thumb brushing her cheek. "But this feels more real than anything I've had in a long time."

He tucked a loose strand of hair behind her ear.

"I'm not asking for forever. Just don't pull away. Not yet."

She nodded, fingers grazing his jaw.

"Okay."

For tonight, it was enough.

For tonight, it was real.

FOURTEEN

SUTTON RECOUNTED THE PREVIOUS night's unexpected developments to Brynn over breakfast in the kitchen. Brynn perched on a barstool like an eager audience member, while Sutton leaned against the island, her fingers tracing the rim of her mug.

"I knew it," Brynn announced, her grin triumphant. "That kiss was bound to happen."

Sutton smiled, a quiet sense of wonder lingering.

"Maybe. It wasn't planned, but it didn't feel shocking either. There's definitely a connection with Wesley."

"Oh, hell yes there is," Brynn whispered, barely containing her delight.

Sutton laughed and leaned in, lowering her voice.

"And between you and me, he's a really good kisser."

Brynn's eyes widened, her reaction cut short only by the awareness that Wesley was somewhere upstairs.

Sutton took a sip of coffee, then added with a mischievous glint,

"And then there's Graham. And we all know Graham is good at everything."

She stretched out the last word deliberately. Brynn gasped, half laughing.

"Well, everything except putting anyone ahead of his work," Brynn countered, giving Sutton a pointed look. "Which reminds me, what's happening with Graham?"

Sutton's expression softened.

"He asked if we could try again. He thinks things would be different this time."

Brynn studied her.

"Are you scared to jump back in?"

Sutton nodded, lips pressing together.

"But I can't ignore what's happening with Wesley. Maybe it's the pull of something new. Or maybe I just don't know yet."

She hesitated, eyes dropping to her mug.

"I'm intrigued by him in ways I didn't expect. But I don't know what this is, or where it could go."

Brynn took a long sip of her coffee.

"So are we talking about cannonballing into Wesley's pool?" She lifted an eyebrow. "Because you sound past the toe-dipping stage."

Sutton groaned, then laughed.

"I'm not all the way in. But yeah. I tested the water, and it was good."

Her laugh faded into a sigh.

"I didn't plan for any of this to happen again this year. Remember when these winter trips had zero complicated men?"

"Please," Brynn said flatly. "That was never real."

After a beat, her tone shifted.

"But honestly, if Wesley weren't around, would you give Graham another chance? Even without him in the picture, it sounds like you're drawn to Wesley."

Sutton chewed her bottom lip. The truth sat there, undeniable.

"Graham hurt me before. And I'm not sure I'm willing to risk that again."

Brynn nodded.

"It sounds like you're wading deeper than you think."

Sutton shot her a look.

Brynn leaned in, her expression gentler now.

"I'm glad you're being thoughtful. Just be honest with yourself. If you're this curious about Wesley, that probably means something."

She hesitated, then added quietly,

"I invited him because he's a good friend. And he's had a rough year mentally. He's in a better place now, but he's not someone who could handle being jerked around. I know you wouldn't hurt him. Just be mindful."

The weight of it settled on Sutton.

"I get it," she said softly. "I won't forget he's human."

***

Upstairs, Wesley lay on his bed, listening to the faint clink of cups and the muted cadence of voices below. He didn't need to guess the subject.

The night before replayed in flashes. The surprise in her eyes. The way she fit against him. The warmth of her hand tucked into his sleeve. Excitement stirred, edged with something heavier. Uncertainty. Hope.

He thought about the age difference. Her life. His chaos. The spotlight. Everything he wasn't sure he could offer. Everything he wasn't sure she would want.

Music was easier. Predictable. Relationships were not. They asked things melodies never did.

With a quiet breath, he pushed off the bed and headed downstairs.

When he appeared in the doorway, both women looked up, their expressions bright with unmistakable guilt.

"Morning," he said.

"Good morning," Brynn replied, entirely too cheerful.

Sutton smiled, equal parts amused and embarrassed.

"So," Wesley said, raising an eyebrow, "last night isn't a secret from Brynn, huh?"

Sutton laughed.

"Nothing ever is. Get used to it."

He chuckled and moved toward the fridge.

"Have either of you eaten yet?"

They shook their heads. Wesley pulled out eggs and vegetables.

"Omelets?" he asked.

Brynn leaned on the island, eyes bright.

"Ah. And he cooks."

"Something I've been inspired to do lately," Wesley said, setting the ingredients out.

He glanced at Sutton, the look warm and unmistakable.

Brynn clapped her hands.

"You know what? I could arrange a date night. Just the two of you."

Sutton froze, eyes widening. The idea landed with a soft jolt. Unexpected, but not unwelcome.

Wesley paused with the knife in his hand, then leaned back against the counter, watching her.

"Nothing like putting us on the spot," Sutton said lightly.

She turned to him. "What do you think?"

He crossed the room, towel slung over his shoulder, and stopped in front of her.

"I think spending time alone with you again sounds like a great idea."

His hand brushed her waist, tentative and flirty. Her stomach fluttered.

"That is," he added, "if you're up for it."

Sutton felt her hesitation melt into something hopeful.

"I think I'd be pretty lucky to score a date with Mr. Wesley Preskott."

Brynn groaned dramatically.

"Yay," she squealed, delighted.

Laughter filled the kitchen, warm and familiar.

Brynn slid off her stool.

"Alright. My matchmaking duties are complete. Now, coffee."

Fifteen

That afternoon, the Winter Wine & Brew Festival turned the snow-dusted park into a holiday postcard.

Strings of warm white lights crisscrossed above the grounds, casting everything in a soft golden glow. Evergreen garlands wrapped around lampposts, dotted with red velvet bows. The air smelled of pine, roasted chestnuts, and mulled spices, with faint holiday music drifting from speakers tucked among the décor.

"Who's brave enough for the blind tasting challenge?" Brynn asked, cheeks flushed from the cold and a half-finished cup of spiced wine.

Marcus stepped in beside her, shoulder brushing hers, a grin already forming.

"You're looking at your champion," he declared, rubbing his gloved hands together.

"Big talk." Brynn narrowed her eyes in mock suspicion. "When I win, remember how cocky you sounded."

"When you win?" Marcus laughed, low and full. "I can already taste victory."

They held each other's gaze for a beat too long, history crackling in the space between them.

Cassie clapped her hands together, her wool mittens making a dull thump.

"As always, this is going to be good."

Peter shook his head.

"I'd join, but I'm not getting between those two."

Everett tugged his scarf tighter, deadpan as always.

"There's a fine line between identifying notes of blackberry and making a complete fool of yourself."

"Save your concern," Brynn said, lifting her chin. "My taste buds have been preparing for this moment."

Marcus huffed out a laugh.

"My palate was born ready."

"You two are impossible," Zoe sighed, though her smile gave her away.

A sommelier appeared with a tray of gleaming glasses, each filled with a deep garnet wine. Brynn and Marcus took their places, exchanged one last challenging look, and lifted their glasses like dueling pistols.

***

Several rounds and no clear winner later, they were both insisting they'd been to right answer, their banter growing more theatrical as everyone else dissolved into laughter. Restless energy rippled through the group, and they eventually drifted away from the tasting booth, fanning out among the vendors.

Wesley lingered at a weathered oak stand, pouring bold red blends, letting the warmth slip down his throat. Twenty feet away, Sutton cradled a dark porter in her hand, the beer the color of polished obsidian. Graham stood at her side and his arm slipped around her waist, fingers pressing with the confidence that came from knowing he'd been there before.

Sutton shifted, creating the smallest sliver of space. Subtle, but real.

From his vantage point, Wesley saw it. He saw the way she moved, not a dramatic rejection, just a quiet boundary. Something tugged low in his chest. Not possessiveness exactly, but awareness.

Sutton's gaze found his, and for a beat, the flow of the festival seemed to blur. Her lips curved in the slightest hint of a smile, an almost imperceptible acknowledgment.

I see you.

At the center of the grounds, Brynn and Marcus were back in motion, circling each other with a second round of tasting flight cards in hand.

"All right," Marcus murmured, leaning in so close his breath warmed her ear. "If I win this time, you're making me breakfast in bed."

Brynn arched a brow over the rim of her glass.

"And if I win?"

"You choose," he said, eyes crinkling. "Though I have a strong suspicion breakfast in bed wouldn't disappoint you either."

"Oh, I'll think of something better," she replied, her voice syrup-smooth. "But we'll see if you're lucky enough to find out."

She took an exaggeratedly slow sip, eyes never leaving his.

"You're assuming I'd ever let you win."

He smirked.

"I know better than to assume anything with you."

Their laughter threaded through the sound of clinking glasses and distant carols; a familiar dance they slipped into every year, as natural as breathing.

Near the handcrafted jewelry booth, Cassie and Zoe appeared at Sutton's elbows like a well-timed rescue squad.

"Come on," Cassie said, looping her arm through Sutton's and tugging gently. "Before Brynn and Marcus wager actual clothing."

Zoe hooked onto Sutton's other side.

"Girls' detour," she declared. "Graham can flirt with the beer guy for a minute."

They steered Sutton toward a row of stalls displaying hammered copper earrings, silver pendants, and rings that caught the late afternoon light.

"Don't tell me you two are back together," Cassie said, fingers brushing over a tray of delicate bracelets that chimed softly.

Zoe nudged Sutton's shoulder, her tone light, not sharp.

"Yeah, give us the status update. Friend vibes? Almost-something? 'It's complicated'?"

Sutton traced the grain of the wooden counter with her thumb, eyes on a tray of simple gold rings.

"I'm trying not to define it yet," she said. "Seeing what feels right first."

"He's hot," Zoe allowed, glancing toward Graham, who was laughing with Everett by a brewery tent, the wind ruffling his dark hair. "And that confidence should come with a warning label."

Then her gaze slid briefly toward Wesley by the wine booth, where he was talking to Marcus, his profile lit by a string of festival lights.

Zoe watched him for a moment, noticing how his attention kept drifting back toward their group even when someone else was speaking.

"I'm pretty sure his attention isn't on Cassie or me," she said quietly. "So it looks like you've got options."

Sutton's stomach tightened, already knowing where Zoe's gaze had landed.

Zoe gave a small shrug, more amused than wounded.

"I dropped a few hints earlier this week," she admitted. "He's sweet. Easy to be around."

Her eyes flicked back toward Wesley as his gaze drifted once again in Sutton's direction.

"But he's already looking somewhere else."

There was no bitterness in her voice. Just simple truth.

Cassie made a small sympathetic sound, then suddenly held up a pendant shaped like a tiny sun.

"Wait. Emergency distraction," she announced. "Tell me that isn't the cutest thing you've ever seen."

"Super cute, you should get it," Sutton said, grateful for the distraction.

They wandered toward a painter's tent, where canvases saturated with color lined the walls. Cassie marched ahead, offering a running commentary about "tourist trap prices," while Zoe hung back with Sutton.

Sutton lingered over a watercolor where lake and sky blurred together in soft lavenders and silvers.

Zoe watched her quietly.

"You should get it," she murmured. "It suits you."

Sutton's fingers tingled as she passed a few bills to the gray-haired artist, accepting the small painting like something fragile. She held it against her chest, breathing in the faint scent of paper and paint.

Cassie spotted another jewelry booth and tugged Zoe away, leaving Sutton alone with her painting and thoughts.

A moment later, Graham slipped in at her side. His presence was familiar, the well-worn sweater of her past, comforting and a little constricting at once.

“You ok, you seem far away,” he observed, his tone light but probing.

“I’m ok,” Sutton said automatically, though even she could hear the thinness in her reply.

Graham let it go for now, but his eyes stayed on her a beat longer.

Cassie wandered back toward them with Zoe close behind, still holding the little sun pendant she’d been admiring. Marcus and Brynn followed a moment later, laughter trailing with them as they drifted toward the wine booth where Wesley stood.

Across the grounds, crew members were setting up a small stage. Musicians tested cables and tuned their instruments, stray notes drifting above the chatter.

A wiry man with a battered guitar slung over his shoulder scanned the crowd and paused.

He leaned toward the drummer, saying something low. The drummer followed his gaze, then broke into a grin.

The guitarist laughed under his breath, shaking his head as if he couldn’t quite believe it.

A moment later he hopped down from the front of the stage and threaded through the crowd toward Wesley.

“Hey, man,” he said, extending a hand, excitement barely contained. “You’re Wesley Preskott, right?”

Wesley nodded, returning the handshake.

“I’m a huge fan,” the guitarist continued. “Didn’t expect to see you here today.”

He gestured toward the stage behind him.

"We're about to start a set. If you felt like jumping in on a song, we'd follow your lead."

The invitation landed softly but unmistakably.

Brynn, Marcus, Zoe, Cassie, Graham, and Sutton all turned toward Wesley, curiosity sharpening into anticipation.

Wesley smiled automatically, polite as ever, but hesitation flickered beneath it. Months had passed since he'd been on any stage. Since he'd stepped away from the version of himself that only existed under a spotlight.

He glanced across the festival grounds, searching.

Then he took a breath.

"Sure," he said finally. "Why not."

He finished the last sip of wine, handed the empty glass to Marcus with a rueful grin, and followed the singer onto the stage. The borrowed guitar settled against his body like something he'd been missing more than he'd allowed himself to admit.

Wesley leaned toward the guitarist and said something quietly. The man's eyebrows shot up before he nodded and turned to the band.

"Alright," the guitarist called to them, grinning.

The first chords of "Fast Car" drifted into the cold evening, familiar and haunting. Wesley's voice wrapped easily around the melody, steady and sure.

The world around Sutton slowed. The lyrics mingled with the bite of the air, the twinkle of lights, the warmth of the porter in her palms. Onstage, Wesley wasn't the quietly observant guy who washed dishes beside her or joked about pie. He was something bigger, an artist completely at home inside the song.

Her heart swelled with pride. But beneath that bloom of feeling, unease stirred.

The phones raised to capture him. The hungry focus of the crowd. The way attention shifted in an instant from casual to consuming.

It was his reality, the orbit he lived in. And hers wasn't.

By the time he reached the last verse, the entire park had gone still. When the last note faded, the applause crashed over him like a wave: cheers, whistles, strangers calling his name.

Sutton stood on the edge of the crowd, arms wrapped around herself, the painting pressed to her chest. The distance between the stage and the snow felt wider than a few yards of frozen ground.

Brynn appeared at her side, linking their arms as if she'd felt the shift.

"Weird, huh?" Brynn said quietly.

Sutton let out a soft, rueful laugh.

"Yeah. Weird."

"You freaking out?" Brynn asked, gentler now.

Sutton watched as a small crowd gathered around Wesley, phones and napkins suddenly appearing in eager hands. He posed for photos, signed whatever was offered, answering everyone with easy charm.

From a distance, he looked perfectly in control.

But she caught the fatigue in his eyes, the way his shoulders held just a touch too much tension.

"I'm just taking it in," Sutton said. "It's a lot."

Brynn squeezed her arm, then released it, giving her space.

By the time Wesley managed to detach himself from the cluster of fans and made his way down the front steps of the stage, his hair was a little mussed, and his cheeks were pink from the cold and the rush of adrenaline.

He scanned the crowd, searching for only one face.

When his gaze found Sutton's, the noise of the festival seemed to soften.

People were already drifting toward him again, offering quick congratulations, clapping him on the shoulder as he made his way back toward the group.

By the time he reached them, the others were still talking over one another about the performance.

"Well," he said, voice warm and a little hoarse, "that was something."

"You were great," Sutton said, and for once she didn't temper the word. Admiration shone plain in her eyes, mixed with a tangle of other things she couldn't quite name.

He caught the flicker of uncertainty beneath it and felt a faint tug of protectiveness.

"Concerned?" he asked gently, tipping his head as he searched her face.

She let out a small laugh, the sound fogging in the cold air between them.

"About what?" she teased. "The fame, or the women still eyeing you like you're dessert?"

There was an edge of honesty under the joke. She wasn't imagining it: the lingering glances, the way a few strangers edged closer, hoping he might drift back into their orbit.

Wesley took a half-step nearer, closing the gap. The noise of the festival swirled around them, but for a moment it felt distant, as if they'd slipped into a quieter pocket of air.

He leaned in, his breath warm against her ear, his words meant only for her.

"Remember," he murmured, low and certain, "it's *you* I'm spending the evening with."

The words slid through her like heat.

She pulled back just enough to meet his eyes, her heart rattling in her chest.

Her voice came out softer than she meant it to.

"You make it really hard not to feel special."

He smiled then, not for the crowd. Just for her.

Sixteen

The evening descended in a soft hush, signaling the start of Sutton and Wesley's first official date. Headlights carved twin ribbons of light across the snow-covered road, the world outside their windshield unfolding like a winter postcard.

Sutton stared out at the frosted pines blurring past, her breath catching when the grand gates appeared, ironwork dusted in snow, flanked by towering evergreens.

"The Alderwyck?" The words slipped out in a whisper, her fingertips brushing the window as though touching a dream. "I've only ever read about this place."

Wesley's lips curved, "I wanted to leave an impression."

Their tires crunched over the long, sweeping driveway, revealing the estate in full twilight glory. Limestone walls rose in elegant lines, every tall window glowing honey-gold against the dusky sky.

An attendant opened Sutton's door, letting in a curl of crisp, pine-scented air. Wesley was already beside her, hand extended, radiating warmth into her chilled fingers.

Before she could speak, his lips brushed hers. The press of his mouth lingered even after he pulled back.

"Ready?" Wesley asked, his voice low, confident.

Sutton exhaled a slow breath, excitement glinting behind her eyes.

"As ready as I'll ever be."

Inside, the Alderwyck felt like stepping into another century. Polished walnut paneling glowed beneath the soft spill of sconces; the air carried the warm scents of beeswax and aged wood. A host led them down hushed corridors where oil paintings watched from gilded frames.

Their private dining room awaited like a secret. Candlelight flickered across damask walls, crystal glasses scattering rainbows across a perfectly dressed table.

Sutton turned in a slow circle, fingertips gliding along the velvet-backed chair.

"How did you arrange this?"

Wesley lifted a shoulder, the gesture easy, though his eyes betrayed quiet pride.

"I had help," he admitted. "I just wanted tonight to feel memorable."

She held his gaze, warmth unfurling in her chest.

"You've outdone yourself, Preskott."

His smile deepened, eyes creasing at the corners.

"I aim high."

Dinner arrived as a five-course ballet of flavors: delicate pastries, velvety sauces, truffle-laced aromas, but the true feast was their conversation. Every topic branched naturally into another, their words weaving a tapestry of shared curiosities and unexpected connections.

Wesley leaned back, turning his wineglass slowly between his fingers.

"Every summer growing up, I'd escape to my grandmother's lake house. There was a massive willow tree hanging over the water. I'd sit under it for hours reading until it got too dark to see."

Sutton rested her chin in her hands, eyes softening.

"That sounds perfect. Peaceful. Yours."

He nodded, gaze distant with nostalgia.

"It was the only place I could breathe without the world tugging at me."

"What book were you obsessed with back then?" she asked.

He chuckled, thumb brushing the rim of his glass.

"The Hobbit. I read it twice one summer. The idea of stepping out of your comfort zone, finding something bigger than you ever expected, really hit me."

"I can see that," she murmured. "A quiet boy dreaming of dragons."

His eyes lifted, steady and searching.

"What about you? Your escape?"

She traced a fingertip along the damask tablecloth.

"I sketched. Constantly. Scenes from books. Imagined cities and moonlit rivers. It was how I held onto things."

He leaned forward, elbows settling on the table.

"Do you still draw?"

Her smile wavered, thinning at the edges.

"Not as much. Life made noise, and it got harder to quiet everything long enough to see the lines."

He studied her with a slow warmth in his gaze.

"You should start again. I'd like to see the world the way you draw it."

Color bloomed across her cheeks.

"Maybe I will."

Between courses, they drifted into dreams of faraway places.

"If you could be anywhere right now," Sutton asked, "where would you choose?"

"Iceland," he said instantly. "Wide-open landscapes, northern lights, the quiet that hums."

She smiled.

"Iceland's on my list, too. Standing under those lights, I imagine it feels like discovering the universe is bigger than your worries."

"Maybe we'll go together," he said softly.

The suggestion wrapped around her like warm wool.

"Your turn."

"Japan," she said. "Temples beside skyscrapers. Cherry blossoms drifting through neon."

His eyes lit.

"I can picture you there. Kyoto at sunrise. Mist in the gardens. It fits you."

Her laugh was soft, delighted.

"Maybe you can be my tour guide."

"Deal."

By the time dessert arrived, time had softened around them. The chocolate soufflé released a burst of cocoa-scented steam as they shared it, spoons clinking lightly.

A host approached and bowed slightly.

"If you're ready, we have a surprise prepared."

Sutton blinked at Wesley in question. He simply stood and offered his hand.

Outside, the terrace overlooked a garden transformed into winter magic. Hundreds of small lights twinkled among snow-draped branches, reflecting off the drifts like scattered stars. A pianist played softly beneath a canopy of evergreens.

Champagne arrived, crisp and icy.

"Champagne is my bloodline," Sutton said with a smile.

"I know," Wesley said, winking.

He stepped behind her, his arm circling her waist. Sutton leaned into him, her cheek warmed by his coat, her body softening in his closeness.

"This feels magical," she whispered.

He rested his chin lightly against her temple.

"It's the kind of night musicians try to write songs about," he murmured, his voice brushing her skin like velvet.

The moment wrapped around them, quiet and impossibly intimate.

"Our bubble," she said softly.

"Our snow globe," he corrected.

Later, in the hushed marble hallway, their footsteps fell into an easy rhythm. Wesley's fingers intertwined with hers, brushing slow circles across her skin.

"Is it time to head back to Brynn's?" she asked quietly, though the reluctance in her voice was clear.

Wesley's grin was slow and knowing.

"If we want," he said softly. "But we don't have to."

Sutton stopped walking and turned toward him, confusion shifting into curiosity.

"What do you mean?"

He stepped closer, dipping his head so his lips grazed her ear.

"It's a hotel," he murmured, warmth spreading across her neck. "We can go back to Brynn's, or we can stay here. Tonight is ours."

The possibility shimmered between them. Candlelight from a nearby sconce cast his expression in gold.

Her heart skipped.

"Really?" she breathed.

"Really."

Her decision rose like a tide, inevitable and certain.

"Then," she said slowly, a smile blooming across her face, "let's not end our night yet."

Relief and desire flashed across his expression. His fingers tightened around hers as he lifted their joined hands to his lips.

"Come on," he said softly.

Seventeen

The suite welcomed them with a grandeur that somehow felt intimate, a private sanctuary tucked high within the estate. Moonlight poured through the twin balconies, casting the snow-dusted gardens in a wash of silver. A fire crackled in the hearth, its glow painting amber shadows that swayed across the walls.

Sutton drifted toward the windows, unable to resist the view. Frost feathered the edges of the glass like delicate lacework, and beyond it the world lay untouched, serene. She exhaled softly, absorbing the quiet beauty, until she sensed him at her back.

Wesley's presence wrapped around her before his arms did, the faint spice of his cologne threading through the air. When he slid his arms around her waist, the warmth of him seeped instantly through the fabric of her dress. In the window's reflection, their silhouettes blended together, two outlines slowly becoming one.

"Wesley..." His name left her lips on a breath she hadn't meant to release. "Tonight's been..."

But the sentence dissolved as his mouth found the curve of her neck. The kiss was slow, unhurried, and heat unfurled through her in a shimmering wave.

She turned in his arms, their faces inches apart, the space between them charged and humming. Her fingertips lifted to his jaw, brushing over the rough shadow of stubble. The texture grounded her, steady and electric all at once. Her hands moved of their own accord, slipping down to the buttons of his shirt with a boldness she didn't stop to question.

One button, then another. Each one revealed a little more warmth, a little more of him. The shirt eased from his shoulders like a secret being shared, and Sutton's breath caught at the sight of his chest rising with quiet, uneven breaths.

Their lips met, deepening with a hunger that surprised them both. She tasted Merlot and something undeniably him as his mouth moved against hers, coaxing, savoring.

Her fingers threaded through the thick strands of his hair, drawing him closer. Wesley's hands found her waist, anchoring her as though he needed the steadiness only she could provide. The heat of his skin bled through her palms, quickening her pulse. His heartbeat thudded beneath her hand where it rested on his chest, syncing with her own.

His mouth traced a line along her jaw, trailing down the warm column of her throat. Each kiss drew a soft, involuntary sound from her lips, her body responding before her mind could catch up.

Wesley's hands skimmed beneath the hem of her dress, his fingertips drawing slow, teasing patterns against her skin. The gentle friction raised goosebumps along her thighs, stealing her breath. She tugged his shirt fully free, her palms roaming the toned lines of his torso, feeling the shift of muscle beneath her touch. When her nails grazed lightly along his ribs, his breath hitched, an unguarded sound that lit something molten and bright inside her.

The midnight-blue dress slipped from her shoulders and fell to the floor. Cool air brushed her skin before Wesley's mouth followed, warm at the hollow of her throat. A shiver ran through her, replaced almost instantly by heat.

He guided her back toward the four-poster bed, its carved frame glowing in the firelight. The cotton sheets were cool against the curve of her spine as she sank into them, breath catching when Wesley hovered above her, all quiet strength and intent.

Their mouths found each other again, deeper this time, their kisses losing any semblance of restraint. His hands moved over her with a surety that unraveled her, mapping the lines of her body as though he'd known them far longer than a single night. Her fingers fumbled at his waistband, earning a soft, hungry sound from him before he shed the last barrier between them.

The fireplace crackled across the room, sparks rising like tiny echoes of the tension building between them. Outside, snow drifted in soft spirals, nature itself slowing to witness the rising heat inside the walls of their secluded suite.

Their breaths synced, their bodies finding an instinctive rhythm, unhurried at first, then deepening with every shared touch. Wesley moved with a focused intensity, his forehead pressed to hers, his hands anchoring her as though afraid she might slip away. Sutton arched into him, her legs tightening around his waist, the gold anklet at her ankle catching and scattering the firelight like a tiny constellation. Their bodies moved in perfect counterpoint, Wesley's narrow hips driving into Sutton with increasing fervor, as her nails skimmed along his back, eliciting a low sound from his throat.

Sutton's cries crescendoed with each powerful stroke, drowning the protesting creaks of the antique bed frame as her body trembled on the precipice of ecstasy. At last, she shattered like fine crystal, her inner walls pulsating rhythmically around his rigid length as white-hot pleasure blazed from her core to her fingertips. The exquisite sensation of her release triggered Wesley's own, and he followed her into oblivion with a guttural groan, his essence spilling in hot pulses deep within her.

Their bodies trembled, slick with sweat, as they collapsed into the tangle of cotton sheets that smelled faintly of jasmine and musk. The once-crisp linens now twisted around their intertwined limbs, warm and damp against their flushed skin.

As they lay entwined in the afterglow, their skin cooling in the amber glow of firelight, Wesley meticulously memorized the trails he'd traced moments ago. His fingers had caressed up

Sutton's thighs, the softness beneath his fingertips sparking a hunger deep inside him. Her body arched at his touch when he brushed against the wet heat between her legs.

Their breathing synced, a slow rise and fall, the shared rhythm grounding them in the room's hush. Wesley rested his forehead against hers, his chest pressing lightly against her palm where she held him close. When he kissed her temple, it was unhurried and tender, an offering more intimate than anything that had come before.

"And to think," he murmured in her ear, voice still rough with leftover heat, "they say the second time's supposed to be better."

Sutton's laugh escaped before she could catch it, warm and breathy against his jaw. The look in his eyes turned her cheeks hot.

"Well," she teased, trailing a finger along the strong line of his jaw, "then I guess we'll have to find out."

His answering chuckle rumbled against her collarbone. Goosebumps shivered down her skin as he pressed a soft kiss to her forehead.

"Challenge accepted," he whispered, his thumb tracing slow, featherlight circles on her shoulder. A simple touch, but it sent sparks racing through every nerve.

They eased deeper into each other, trading soft kisses and almost-there touches, memorizing the shape of the moment. The sheets whispered beneath them, wrapping them in a private world that felt suspended, untouched.

Beyond the balcony doors, winter settled over the garden. Moonlight spilled across the floor in pale ribbons. Dawn would come eventually, but for now, the night held them gently.

Wesley's voice broke the quiet, low and unsteady.

"Whatever happens after tonight..." His arms tightened around her, drawing her close until she felt the steady drum of his heart beneath her palm. "This—" His breath stumbled. "This is the most real thing I've felt in a long time. And that terrifies me."

Sutton lifted her head, their faces only inches apart. Vulnerability flickered across his features. It mirrored the fragile bloom of hope inside her, soft but impossible to ignore.

She cupped his cheek and kissed him, tasting of promises she wasn't ready to voice but couldn't deny. When she pulled back, her lips still tingled.

"Me too," she whispered.

Eighteen

Crisp morning air settled in the quiet bedroom as Sutton stirred, consciousness returning slowly beneath warm sheets. The warmth beside her anchored her before she even opened her eyes.

She turned, and her breath stalled.

Wesley slept next to her, peaceful and unguarded. Morning light poured across his features, softening every angle. His chest rose and fell in a steady, quiet rhythm, and for a suspended moment, she simply watched him.

This was real.

Careful not to wake him, she slipped from the bed. Goosebumps prickled her skin as she wrapped herself in a robe and padded toward the balcony doors. Outside, fresh snow glittered under the pale morning sun; a world washed clean, untouched, new.

Fabric rustled behind her.

She turned quickly and found Wesley leaning against the doorway, hair tousled, eyes soft with sleep.

"You're up early," he murmured.

"Habit," she said. "Sorry, did I wake you?"

He shook his head and crossed the balcony toward her.

"Let me guess," he said with a light smirk. "Thinking about last night?"

Heat rushed up her neck.

"Something like that."

A low laugh escaped him, warm enough to melt frost.

"Good thoughts, I hope."

"Mostly," she teased, though they both knew the truth.

He reached for her hand, their fingers threading together easily.

"Don't overthink it. Last night was..." He exhaled, searching for the right word. "New. Good."

She swallowed.

"Just good?" she asked, uncertainty slipping into her voice. "This isn't the part where you tell me it was a huge mistake so we can do the awkward morning-after thing?"

Wesley shook his head immediately.

"No regrets. Not a single one."

She let out a breath she hadn't realized she'd been holding.

"That's good to hear," she said with a small smile. "With where I am in my life, I don't really have the luxury of pretending anymore."

His expression softened, his attention settling fully on her.

"We don't have to pretend anything," he said. "I mean it when I say I'm not going anywhere. Not unless you tell me to."

Sutton turned her gaze toward the glittering gardens below, her hands curling around the cold railing.

"Every good thing I've ever trusted disappears the second I believe in it."

He stepped closer.

"Well, I'm not making promises I can't keep," he said quietly. "I'm just telling you what I want. And I want to stay."

He paused until she looked back at him, making sure she understood.

"With you. Whatever this is. Even if it gets messy or complicated or terrifying."

A shaky breath left her, visible in the cold air.

"And what if I wake up tomorrow and decide this was a terrible idea?"

He nudged her shoulder gently, warmth rolling off him.

"Then I'll be the worst idea you can't shake."

A surprised laugh slipped out of her, small but real.

He squeezed her hand, thumb brushing soft strokes across her knuckles.

"We don't need to figure out the next year," he murmured. "Or even next week. We just take baby steps. Then the one after that."

Wesley tilted his head, giving her that crooked half-smile that could undo her instantly.

"Coffee?" he asked lightly, as if the ground hadn't shifted beneath them overnight.

She lifted a brow, heat blooming low in her stomach.

"Or," she whispered, stepping closer, "we skip breakfast and make this morning even better than last night."

Wesley's grin was slow, devastating. His eyes darkened.

"Sutton..."

Before he could finish, she hooked a finger into the collar of his robe and tugged him back inside, the balcony door closing softly behind them.

He laughed, as she backed him toward the bed.

"Second-time theory, huh?" he murmured against her mouth.

A smile curved her lips.

"Only fair."

His gaze darkened, pupils widening. He reached for her, but she caught his wrists.

"Not yet," she whispered, pinning his hands to the mattress.

He groaned, a delicious mix of surrender and hunger, as his head fell back, throat exposed, muscles lounging in anticipation.

As she straddled him, her thighs settled around his hips, and she slid her hands across his chest. She planted a series of kisses along his jaw, teeth grazing skin, drawing a quivering shudder from him.

Sutton set a deliberate rhythm, hips moving with tantalizing precision. Wesley's hands gripped her thighs, fingers pressing into soft flesh with worshipful pressure.

"You're dangerous," he said reverently.

She leaned in, hair fanning around them, a slow, wicked smile curving her lips.

"You have no idea."

He inhaled sharply, chest rising and falling under her touch. He trailed fingers down her side, then tangled them in her hair, tugging gently.

When their lips met again, it was urgent, commanding, yet tender; a shock of pleasure that bound them together.

She sped up her movement, every roll of her hips demanding more. His grip tightened on her skin, knuckles whitening as his control slipped.

Their bodies moved as one, a pulse of tension building with each breath.

She arched back, eyes fluttering shut as a shattering wave rolled through her. Her soft cries echoed in the room, muscles quivering in release.

He followed, anchoring her with his hands as his own climax tore through him, a low, raw, trembling beneath her.

They stayed suspended in that heated moment, breaths mingling, hearts pounding as their bodies finally stilled. Sutton collapsed forward, palms splayed across Wesley's chest, feeling the rise and fall of his slowing breath beneath her hands.

Her fingers traced idle shapes across his warm skin, the quiet between them settling like a soft blanket.

"That was..." She tried to speak, but her voice caught halfway.

Wesley finished for her, his lips grazing her temple as he breathed the words against her skin, low and rough with satisfaction.

"Fucking good."

A helpless, breathless laugh escaped her before she could catch it.

"Careful," she murmured, shifting just enough to meet his eyes. "Talk like that, and you'll never want to leave."

His smile spread, wicked at the edges, warm at the center.

"Among the many reasons," he whispered against her mouth.

She rolled onto her back with a contented sigh, stretching across the pillows as sunlight slid over her bare shoulder. Wesley mirrored her movement, hair adorably tousled, breathing still uneven, the sheets rustling like they knew exactly what had happened in them.

After a quiet beat, he nudged her foot with his, lazy and playful.

"So," he drawled, voice still rasped from sleep and everything they'd just done, "are you planning to keep me hostage in this bed all day, or have you actually worked up an appetite?"

Sutton pushed up on one elbow and poked his chest with a single, decisive finger.

"I demand pancakes," she announced. "And bacon. An irresponsible amount of bacon."

Her lips curving into a grin.

"I need to replenish my strength."

He laughed and tugged her in for one more kiss.

“Pancakes it is,” he murmured against her lips.

Sutton settled back onto the pillows, watching him stretch, muscles bunching under the morning light, his grin easy and boyish, his presence soft and dangerously comfortable.

Sometime between last night and this morning, something had shifted.

And she wasn’t entirely sure she was ready for how real it felt.

Nineteen

When Sutton, Wesley, and Brynn stepped into Marcus's house, holiday magic enveloped them immediately. Pine and mulled wine perfumed the air, wrapping around them like a warm blanket. The mouthwatering aroma of rosemary-crusted lamb and baked apples drifted from the kitchen. Laughter mingled with the soft clink of glasses, rising and falling in a familiar symphony of celebration.

A towering Christmas tree glittered in the corner, its branches heavy with ornaments that threw golden sparks across the room whenever someone passed. Crimson and gold linens dressed the tables, candles casting playful shadows over polished silverware. Classic carols floated through the space, weaving seamlessly with the chatter.

Marcus appeared wearing a reindeer headband and a necklace of blinking lights over a crisp button-down, radiating pure festive energy.

"Hello, hello!" he boomed.

Sutton leaned in to kiss his cheek.

"Every year, you outdo yourself."

Marcus's gaze snagged on Brynn.

"It's perfect." She nudged him lightly. "Your mom was always the queen of hosting parties. Looks like you learned something."

He laughed, nostalgia creeping in.

"Learned something? She trained me as if I were going for Olympic gold."

Brynn's fingers brushed his arm.

"Well, it shows. She'd be proud."

Sutton caught Wesley's eye, the amused quirk of his smile telling her he was enjoying the show.

"I think Marcus might have more Christmas spirit than anyone I've ever met," Wesley murmured, his breath warm against her ear.

"He's definitely a contender," she whispered back.

Marcus caught the whisper and clapped dramatically.

"Alright, no lingering in the entryway. There's food, drinks, and at least three questionable decisions waiting to be made."

Sutton shrugged out of her coat, laughter rippling through the room as everyone began drifting toward the kitchen.

Before she could follow, Graham stepped up beside her, a glass of wine already in his hand. He held it out, his smile easy, familiar.

"Thought you might want this."

She accepted it, their fingers brushing briefly.

"Can we talk for a minute?" he asked quietly.

The house pulsed with music and conversation, but something in his tone created a small pocket of calm between them. Sutton hesitated, then gave a small nod.

Graham gestured down the hallway rather than taking the lead outright. Together they moved toward a frosted window where ice crystals framed the glass like lace.

"You look beautiful tonight," he said, his gaze tracing the line of her red dress with open appreciation.

"Thank you." She smiled. "You look pretty good yourself." She gave him a small wink.

He reached out, his fingers catching lightly at the fabric at her waist in a playful tug.

"Tonight's my last night here. I have to head back into the city for work." He looked disappointed but hopeful. "I wanted to see if you'd thought more about what we talked about."

Under the dim glow of the hallway sconces, the weight of their history pressed in. Memories filled with warmth, hurt, and distance flickered through her.

"I haven't had time to really sit with it," she admitted. She gestured faintly around them. "And this isn't where I want to figure it out."

He exhaled, his shoulders dropping slightly.

"So it's not a no?"

Her voice softened. "It's a conversation for real life, not here. Last time the bubble felt perfect, and then everything collapsed the second we got home. I'm not going to make a choice in this fantasy space."

The small spark of hope in his expression twisted something inside her.

"I just wanted to know where your head was," he said quietly.

"Graham," she said, steady but kind, "let's wait. Please."

He nodded slowly, trying and failing to hide the disappointment tightening his jaw.

Across the house, Wesley hovered near the mantel with a bourbon in hand, laughter from Peter and Zoe swirling around him. Brynn drifted close and jabbed his ribs lightly.

"You've got that look," she said, raising a brow.

"What look?"

"The look of a man pretending he didn't just watch his girl talk to another guy."

Wesley choked on his drink.

"She's not my girl."

Brynn gave him a long, knowing look.

"Mm-hmm. And I'm not wearing glitter reindeer antlers."

He cracked a reluctant smile.

"I'm just taking it one step at a time."

Brynn's sharp edges softened.

"I didn't invite you hoping you'd end up in whatever this is," Brynn admitted quietly. "But Sutton guarding her heart isn't a personality trait. It's a survival skill. If she's opening even a crack for you, that's rare."

Wesley looked down at his glass, swirling the amber liquid. When he spoke, his voice was quieter.

"I wasn't out here searching for anyone either."

"Yeah," she said softly, glancing across the room at Sutton. "That's usually how the real things start."

She bumped his shoulder again, gentler this time.

"Stop thinking so hard. Let it be what it is."

Marcus's voice suddenly boomed through the room, dramatic as ever.

"Okay, now that everyone has arrived, dinner is officially served!"

The room erupted in cheers, and conversations fractured into warm, hungry motion.

Dinner unfolded in a cozy haze of laughter and clinking silverware. Candles flickered against crystal glasses, throwing gold across faces flushed from wine and warmth. Marcus brought out the rosemary lamb with performative flair, Zoe nearly dropped an entire bowl of mashed potatoes on Peter's lap, and Brynn teased Marcus about his "chef voice," which he insisted was real and not at all pretentious.

Wesley sat beside Sutton, close enough for their knees to brush beneath the table when they both reached for the bread basket. Every accidental touch felt charged, little sparks stitching themselves into her awareness.

Conversation layered over itself: holiday plans, travel mishaps, disastrous work stories. Wesley loosened under it all, laughing more freely than Sutton had heard him in weeks, storytelling with an effortless charm that pulled even Graham into the orbit of his humor.

Dessert appeared.

Wine refilled.

Laughter deepened.

And when the last plates were whisked away, Marcus clinked a spoon against his glass with dramatic gusto, his grin wide and mischievous.

"Alright," he announced, rising from his chair, "now that we're fed, tipsy, and mildly sentimental, it's time for true chaos. White Elephant begins!"

The table erupted again, voices lifting in playful anticipation as everyone pushed back their chairs and the sleepy comfort of dinner gave way to a brighter, rowdier energy.

The opening notes of "Have Yourself a Merry Little Christmas" filled the room, Wesley's recorded voice threading through the melody.

Wesley groaned.

"Marcus..."

Marcus beamed.

"What's a party without humiliating one of our guests of honor?"

Wesley muttered, "You'll pay for this."

"Promises, promises," Marcus shot back.

"Who's number one?" he called.

"That's me," Wesley said, lifting his hand.

Sutton leaned in.

"Pick the one with the ridiculous bow."

He smirked.

"Are you trying to sabotage me?"

"Maybe."

He tore open the box and held up two miniature plastic hands.

"Emergency Tiny Hands," he read flatly.

Marcus cackled.

"We officially ban you from normal-sized tasks for the rest of the night!"

The game continued with playful competition. Brynn claimed a luxury candle set from Marcus, who immediately retaliated by stealing Everett's whiskey. Zoe vanished beneath an oversized blanket, only her triumphant eyes peeking out as she proclaimed herself the evening's undisputed champion.

When the last gift changed hands, a peaceful quiet settled over the room, the kind that follows shared laughter and full stomachs. The evening wrapped around them like a soft, well-worn sweater. Faces glowed pink from wine and merriment beneath the tree's constellation of tiny lights.

By the time midnight crept closer, the party's vibrant pulse gentled, its energy ebbing like a slow tide.

The fire had melted to embers, casting just enough golden light to illuminate wine-drowsy faces leaning closer in conversation. Laughter still sparked here and there, but hushed now, intimate.

Zoe set down her glass with a soft clink.

"Last night already for some of us."

She leaned into Peter, her hair spilling over his shoulder like a spill of copper.

Brynn raised her glass toward Cassie, a teasing smile tugging at her lips.

"Some of us aren't rushing back to cubicles just yet."

Everett checked his watch and began to stand up.

"Speaking of which, I should head out. Eight a.m. flight."

He clasped Marcus's hand, their palms lingering a beat longer than a simple goodbye.

"Next December?"

"Wouldn't miss it," Marcus replied. The smile that followed threaded through the softness of tradition.

Zoe rose next, her steps reluctant beneath her bright expression. She pulled Brynn into a fierce hug.

"Real life awaits," she murmured into Brynn's hair. "Text me?"

"Count on it."

As she passed, Wesley offered a calm smile.

"Stay out of trouble."

Zoe shot him a crooked grin.

"No guarantees."

Peter patted his pockets, wobbling only slightly.

"Shall we retreat to our humble abode? This wine has me seeing double."

Cassie jingled her keys triumphantly and wrestled with her coat.

"Already ahead of you."

Peter laughed, shoulders sagging with exhaustion.

"Remember when I could drink a bottle and still ski black diamonds?"

Cassie arched a brow.

"Speaking of slopes, tomorrow?"

Marcus and Brynn answered in perfect unison.

The cabin door closed with a soft click behind them, sealing the cool air outside and ushering in a hush that felt like an exhale.

Half the group was gone now: called back to airports, obligations, the slowly creeping reality of everyday life. But those who remained stood suspended in the warm afterglow of the night, instinctively leaning into the comfort of each other and the last days of their winter retreat.

The moment lingered, tender in a way that made it feel like the trip's very heart.

Twenty

Wesley lay beside Sutton in the amber glow of morning, studying the gentle rise and fall of her breath beneath the rumpled sheets. Lavender clung faintly to the air, warm and comforting, blending with the softness of sleep lingering between them. He brushed a stray strand of hair from her cheek, watching it shimmer in the sunlight.

Sutton stirred, nestling closer into his warmth. Her lips curved instinctively before her eyes even opened.

"Morning," she murmured, her voice thick with sleep, warm breath feathering over his throat.

"Morning."

Wesley leaned in, pressing a slow kiss to her lips. When he pulled back, he let his gaze linger, memorizing every delicate shift in her features.

"I could get used to this," he said quietly, shifting closer until the mattress dipped beneath his weight.

The smallest shadow crossed her face, fleeting, enough for him to catch it.

"A few days left," she whispered, the words landing between them like a snowflake that somehow thudded.

Wesley found her hand underneath the covers, threading his fingers through hers. His thumb traced slowly, grounding circles against her palm.

"It doesn't have to end," he said, voice steady despite the pulse nudging faster in his neck. "The bubble doesn't have to burst the second we go home."

Sutton sat up, the sheet pooling at her waist. She tucked a strand of hair behind her ear, the crease between her brows deepening.

"What do you mean?"

He hesitated only a beat before diving in.

"I've kept a place in New York. Quiet. Hardly anyone knows about it. I could stay there for a while. We could have time. Real time. To figure out whatever this is."

The morning, which moments ago had felt soft and warm, suddenly sharpened with possibility.

"You'd do that? For me?"

Wesley tugged her hand gently back into his, grounding her before her doubt could spiral.

"For us," he corrected, his voice low but certain. "No timeline. No pressure. We just take this one day at a time and see where it leads."

Her heartbeat fluttered visibly at the base of her throat. She looked down, staring at their joined hands as if the answer hid in the spaces between their fingers.

"It feels like a lot, Wesley," she confessed softly. "You're always moving. I'm—" she exhaled. "I'm afraid of trusting something that could disappear."

He squeezed her hand, leaning in close enough that the warmth wrapped around her like a blanket.

"Then it disappears," he said gently. "Or it doesn't. But I don't want fear to make the decision for us. Not when we haven't even tried. Do you?"

She lifted her eyes to his, vulnerability swimming beneath her hazel irises.

"No," she whispered. "I don't want to give up before we try either."

Relief broke across his face. He pressed a kiss to her forehead, lingering there like a vow sealed in warmth.

"One step at a time," he echoed against her skin.

***

Winter sunlight glazed the park in icy gold as Sutton and Brynn walked side by side, their boots crunching through fresh powder. Their breath rose in soft clouds, dissolving into the brittle air. Bare branches arched overhead as cathedral spires etched against the pale sky.

"So," Brynn said lightly, though her eyes gleamed with unmistakable intent, "I saw you and Graham talking yesterday. What's the situation?"

Sutton let out a long breath, watching it dissipate.

"He left early this morning. We said we'd talk when we're both back in the city, but..."

She shrugged.

"It felt like a placeholder. Something you promise out of habit, not hope."

Brynn linked her arm through Sutton's, guiding them along a path dappled with sunlight and shadow.

"So what does that mean?" she pressed.

A small smile tugged at Sutton's lips, brightening her face in the thin winter light.

"It means..." She inhaled, excitement threading through the quiet. "It means I have space to explore other possibilities."

Brynn practically bounced.

"Other possibilities. I love that phrase."

They passed a frozen fountain, icicles suspended mid-drip like glass teeth. A cardinal flashed red against the white landscape before flitting away.

"Speaking of possibilities," Brynn said, voice rising, "tell me about you and Wesley. I need details. Preferably all of them."

Heat climbed Sutton's cheeks.

"The date was magical. It felt like stepping into a dream I didn't realize I'd been wanting."

She paused, her breath coming out in a slow, visible exhale.

"We didn't plan to stay over," she admitted softly. "But with Wesley? Nothing felt forced. Not for one moment."

Brynn's grin widened with uncontained delight.

"Look at you. Another winter, another plot twist."

Sutton laughed, nudging her shoulder.

"It's not like that. With Graham, everything always felt intense. Like I was moving forward on a track that was already laid for us. With Wesley, it's lighter. It breathes."

Her fingers drifted toward her phone in her pocket, almost unconsciously.

"What's going to happen?" Brynn asked as they neared a bench dusted with snow. "Have you talked about after the trip?"

Sutton slowed, chewing her lip.

"He said he could stay in New York for a while. That he wants to see where this goes."

Brynn stopped cold, boots crunching.

"Wait. Hold up. He said that? Sutton, this isn't a casual winter fling. That's big."

"It is big," Sutton admitted, voice thin with nerves. "And terrifying."

The wind rustled the bare branches overhead, showering them with soft flakes of frost.

"Let's talk about the neon sign you keep avoiding," Brynn said gently. "Wesley isn't exactly an anonymous guy. How do you feel about all of that?"

Sutton's breath puffed unevenly in the cold.

"It's a lot. Being with him means stepping into a world I never planned for. The attention, the scrutiny. All of it."

"Does the age difference still worry you?" Brynn asked.

"Sometimes," Sutton admitted. "Eight years feels like nothing and everything all at once. I worry our timelines won't line up, especially if I decide I want kids someday."

Brynn nodded.

"But you don't have to decide any of that today."

Sutton looked up at the sky, pale and endless.

"For once, I just want to enjoy the good without dissecting it. I feel special with him. Chosen. Is that so wrong?"

Brynn elbowed her lightly.

"Of course not. Love is messy. But if you're lucky, the mess is where the magic is."

Sutton laughed softly.

"Only you could make chaos sound romantic."

"That's why you keep me around," Brynn said brightly. "Stop trying to see the entire picture right now. Just find the corner pieces. Build from there."

Sutton's tension eased, like warmth spreading into cold fingers.

"You're right." She smiled. "When did you become the wise one? Aren't you allergic to commitment?"

Brynn snorted.

"Oh, absolutely. But even a commitment-phobe knows when something is worth leaning toward."

She tugged Sutton close, looping their arms again.

"And this? With Wesley? It might actually be something."

Twenty-One

The truck's engine growled as Marcus rolled to a stop at the base of the hill. The four doors flew open almost simultaneously, unleashing everyone into the sharp winter air. The cold slapped their cheeks, crisp and invigorating, layered with the clean scent of pine and untouched snow. Their boots crunched as they grabbed sleds from the truck bed, the plastic scraping loudly against metal.

Wesley squinted up at the long, gleaming slope.

"This is it?" he asked, incredulous.

Marcus slapped the side of the truck with a flourish, the sound echoing into the quiet clearing.

"Oh yeah. Look at that incline. Perfect. Steep enough to fly, not steep enough to die."

A beat.

"Probably."

Brynn tugged her wool hat lower until her breath puffed in white clouds.

"Translation: Marcus is dying for someone to chicken out so he can hold it over them for the next ten years."

"Exactly."

Marcus lobbed a sled at her; the plastic cut through the air.

"You're going first."

Brynn caught it with a grunt.

"Rude. But I'll go first. I beat you before; don't think I won't do it again."

Sutton tightened her gloves, feeling the snug elastic at her wrists as she eyed the hill. It wasn't terrifying, but it was tall enough to spark a low thrum of adrenaline beneath her ribs.

"Cassie and Peter missed out," she said.

Wesley's fingers curled around a crimson sled.

"Peter missed out. Cassie's probably thrilled she's not stuck hiking up a hill while he tries to reenact the Winter Olympics."

Sutton laughed, breath misting.

"Less talking, more sledding!" Brynn called halfway to the top already.

They trudged upward, boots sinking deep into fresh powder. The forest stretched around them, towering evergreens shedding glittering snow, sunlight slicing through branches gold.

At the summit, Brynn planted her sled at the edge.

"Watch and learn, losers!"

She shoved off with a triumphant whoop, her sled carving a sharp trail. She spun at the bottom in a spray of snow, popped up, and bowed.

"Beat that!"

Marcus cracked his knuckles.

"Challenge accepted."

He nudged Wesley.

"Your turn, rock star."

Wesley didn't hesitate. He sprinted forward, dropped onto his sled, and launched. Halfway down, he hit a bump and soared, arms flung out like a kid, before landing with a satisfying thud.

Sutton clapped, laughter spilling freely as Wesley took an exaggerated bow.

Marcus grinned.

"All right. Sutton's up next."

She stepped forward, but Marcus blocked her gently with his arm. His playful expression wavered, giving way to something quieter.

"I like him," he said, low.

Sutton blinked.

"Marcus..."

He raised a hand.

"I'm a vibe guy, Sutton. And right now, the vibe between you two is screaming at full volume."

A laugh escaped her, soft and unsure.

"So, you like him?"

Marcus shrugged, the sled creaking as he leaned against it.

"Yeah. He's cool. But he's not..."

He paused, searching for the right word.

"He's not like us."

The wind picked up, carrying pine and cold across her cheeks.

“It’s tours, cameras, fans, headlines,” Marcus said quietly. “It’s a lot. And you…”

He tapped her chest lightly.

“You like your life steady. Peaceful. Being with Wesley, it won’t always be quiet.”

Sutton swallowed.

“I’m not jumping in blind. We’re taking it slow.”

Marcus’s face softened.

“I know. But you don’t do anything halfway. If you let this get real, it'll be real. Then you’ll have to face the parts of his world that don’t fit yours.”

She looked down the hill where Wesley stood, laughing with Brynn.

“I’ve thought about all of that,” she whispered. “I can’t pretend it’s not scary. But I also can’t pretend I don’t feel what I feel.”

Marcus exhaled, his breath a white cloud.

“I just want you to be careful. You’re too good to lose yourself in someone else’s chaos.”

Before Sutton could respond, a voice rang out

“What are you two doing? Let’s go!”

Brynn’s shout echoed through the clearing.

Sutton laughed, the heaviness easing just slightly.

Marcus nudged her sled toward her.

“Race you down?”

She grinned.

“Prepare to lose.”

They pushed off at the same moment, sleds hissing over snow, laughter flying behind them like a trail of sparks.

***

The last night of the winter retreat fell quietly, wrapping the cabin and the snowy trees outside in a softness that felt almost sacred. Wesley and Sutton slipped into Brynn’s empty house. The lingering scent of pine and cinnamon drifted through the air, warm reminders of all the nights they had shared within its walls.

Sutton unwound her scarf, fingers brushing over the wool as if reluctant to let go of something familiar. She draped her coat over a chair and exhaled. Wesley watched her, noting the subtle tension in her jaw, the tightness in her shoulders that didn’t belong there.

He stepped closer, his hand finding the small of her back in a gentle, grounding touch.

“Sit with me.”

The leather sofa sighed beneath her weight as she sank down. Wesley remained standing for a moment, the lamp casting long, gold-tinted shadows behind him. The house ticked and hummed around them, quiet in a way that asked for honesty.

Finally, he crouched in front of her and took her hands.

"It's our last night here," he said softly. "You've been quiet all evening. Talk to me."

Sutton swallowed, her gaze fixed on their intertwined fingers. When she spoke, her voice trembled.

"I'm scared. I want this. I want to try with you. But everything feels so uncertain."

Wesley's features gentled, every sharpness softening.

"I'm scared too."

The admission steadied her more than any reassurance could have.

Sutton drew a slow breath, the crisp winter air still clinging faintly to their clothes.

"When I think about the future," she said, "I see a home. A partner. And someday, maybe kids." Her voice wavered. "Not now, not soon, but someday. And if we're going to try this, then I need to know if that's something you could want, too."

Wesley didn't blink. His gaze held hers.

"I've seen the world. Lived in too many cities. Poured myself into music until it almost broke me. I know what I want now."

He lifted his hand, brushing his thumb across her cheek with aching tenderness.

"No, I'm not ready for cribs and midnight feedings tomorrow. But with someone who matters? Sure, I can picture that someday."

Her inhale stuttered, barely there.

"But what if this is just a moment?" she whispered. "A beautiful moment in a bubble that bursts the second we leave."

Wesley cupped her face with both hands, his palms warm against her chilled skin.

"Sutton, I'd rather have one extraordinary moment with you than a lifetime wondering what we could've been."

Her chest tightened, fear and longing tangled into something fragile and real.

"I can't do a half-connection," she said. "I can't do something destined to fall apart."

"Then don't." His voice cracked, quiet and raw. "Let's give this a chance before fear kills it."

He exhaled shakily.

"I can't say goodbye tonight. If I go back to California tomorrow, this won't survive. We both know that. I need to stay in New York. I need to be where you are."

Her heart thudded painfully at the vulnerability in his eyes.

He shook his head softly.

"We deserve a chance to heal what hurt us in our past. This is our chance to see if this is something real."

Silence settled between them, broken only by the faint crackle of the cooling fireplace.

Then, finally, she whispered.

"Okay."

Wesley's breath caught.

"Okay?"

She nodded, a slow smile blooming at the edges.

"Let's do New York together."

The tension melted out of his body all at once: relief, joy, disbelief, flickering across his face before he leaned in and pressed a kiss to her forehead, soft as a promise.

Sutton closed her eyes and let the decision sink deep into her bones.

For once, she didn't analyze. Didn't brace for disappointment.

She chose hope.

She chose him.

Twenty-Two

"So, we're clear on the plan?" Wesley had asked that morning, breath fogging softly between them. "Just four days apart."

Sutton replayed that moment as she sank into her desk chair. The familiar leather creaked beneath her, grounding her back in her weekday reality. Phones rang, keyboards clacked, and the office buzzed with pre-holiday frenzy, a stark contrast to the serene snow and candlelit dinners of the retreat.

Her phone vibrated against the polished wood surface. Before she could look, a sharp voice cut through her thoughts.

"Earth to Sutton!"

Mark deposited a file directly onto her keyboard with a dramatic thud. His cologne, aggressively citrus, preceded him by two seconds.

"How was the trip?" he asked, leaning a hip against her desk. "Or should I say, who was on the trip?"

His eyebrows lifted meaningfully.

Sutton nudged the folder aside. "Not now, Mark."

But the small, reluctant smile tugging at her mouth gave her away.

Click. Click. Click.

Valentina swept into the doorway, posture so straight it rivaled a runway model's.

"Sutton," she said briskly, already turning. "Glad you're back. The Clarkson gala expanded. Fifty more guests, plus new menus, seating charts, and logistics. I need updated plans by the end of the day."

"I'm on it," Sutton said, already straightening.

Valentina vanished in a trail of expensive perfume. Mark gave a low whistle.

"Welcome back to the circus," he muttered before heading off, his stack of files teetering.

Sutton exhaled and opened her inbox. Messages piled up like snowdrifts.

But beneath it all, her mind drifted relentlessly toward Wesley. Somewhere hundreds of miles away, he was dismantling pieces of his life to rebuild closer to hers.

Her phone buzzed again.

Wesley: ***Miss you.***

Attached: a chaotic selfie of him mid-packing, a mountain of clothes spilling from an open suitcase behind him.

A laugh escaped her, soft and involuntary.

Before she could respond, another notification lit the screen.

Graham: ***Hey, back in town?***

Her stomach tightened. She hadn't expected him to reach out so soon.

She typed:

Yeah, got back this weekend. How are you?

His reply was quick.

Busy as always. Coffee sometime?

The casual tone didn't fool her.

She chewed her lip, then crafted her message carefully:

I'm swamped with work right now. Holiday season madness. Maybe after the holidays?

She waited a few second before his reply came quick:

Sure. I get it. After the holidays.

A quiet exhale slipped from her.

Another buzz.

This time from Wesley. **Four days, Sutton. I can't wait.**

Warmth spread through her chest.

She set her phone down, her decision settling into place like ice forming on a still pond. This was something she chose.

And whether she was ready for it or not, it was happening.

***

Sutton curled into the soft leather of a corner cafe chair, the one she always picked when she needed to breathe. She pulled out her small sketchbook, not to draw anything serious, just to let her pencil wander the way it often did when her mind was too full. Abstract shapes, the curve of a shoulder, the outline of a window she'd glimpsed on her walk over. She hadn't drawn in years. But the familiar glide of graphite steadied her heartbeat.

Her latte steamed beside her, fogging the window. Outside, New Yorkers pushed forward with purpose. Toward their own projects. Their own passions.

Her phone buzzed.

Valentina: ***Excellent work on the Carlsons' affair.***

Rare. Almost unheard of. Sutton should've felt weightless.

She read the email twice.

Flawless.

Impressive.

Well done.

The praise warmed her, but didn't settle. Not the way it once had.

Instead of accomplishment, she felt drift. Like she was excelling at something she'd never meant to build a life around. Something she was good at, but not moved by.

She closed the sketchbook softly, fingertips lingering over the charcoal smudge on her thumb. *Remember this,* she told herself. *This is the part you've been ignoring.*

She slipped on her coat and stepped into the cold.

Three blocks later, she froze in front of a small gallery she'd passed a dozen times. She'd always meant to go in. *Someday,* she'd said to Brynn once, after showing her the sketch she hid in the back of her planner. *Someday,* she'd tell herself on long commutes, passing the same storefronts her life never allowed room for.

Today, the name on the glass felt like an invitation.

Inside, silence wrapped around her like velvet. Paint-laced air. Cold concrete beneath her boots. She drifted between canvases, letting the colors fill the space her job often drained.

A painting caught her breath, the couple beneath a rain-soaked umbrella, faces blurred, bodies leaning together like gravity had chosen them. Color streaked down the canvas in bold, imperfect drips.

It was about connection.

About truth.

About the kind of art she used to dream of curating.

Her chest clenched quietly, painfully.

She had spent years designing perfect spaces for other people's visions. But what about her own? What about the girl who once filled sketchbooks, who'd whispered to Brynn after too much wine, *"One day I'll curate a small show. Something intimate. Something that means something to someone."*

Her phone warmed her palm.

She didn't call Maya right away. She walked the length of the gallery twice, then sat on the bench in the center, letting the idea settle instead of pouncing. Let it feel familiar, not impulsive. Letting her heart answer the question her career never asked:

What if now is 'someday'?

Finally, with breath steady and decision quiet but sure, she dialed.

"Maya? It's Sutton."

A beat.

"I'm thinking about hosting a small, curated art showcase. Local artists. Intimate, not flashy. Could we talk about using your warehouse space?"

This time, the certainty in her voice didn't surprise her. It felt like remembering something she'd nearly forgotten;high l something that had always belonged to her.

By the time she stepped back onto the street, twilight had washed Manhattan in lavender. The city seemed softer, newly aligned with her own pulse.

Three days until Wesley returned.

Three months until she built something that finally felt like hers.

Twenty-Three

Wesley leaned back into the plush leather seat of his jet, the steady drone of the engines a counterpoint to the noise in his head. Outside the oval window, New York's skyline rose through thin wisps of cloud, steel and glass cutting into the winter light. Each skyscraper caught the sun like a shard of an old life.

The city had seen almost everything: sold-out arenas, sleepless studio nights, headlines that blurred until they meant nothing. Today, as the familiar silhouette sharpened, it promised something different.

He lifted his afternoon iced coffee. The scent curled through the cabin's filtered air as his thoughts drifted to Sutton.

The little rasp in her laugh when something genuinely delighted her. The way she listened because it was him speaking, not because of who he was.

While he was in New York, he was also getting some work done. Meetings for his foundation, a few tentative album conversations with producers, and required check-ins his manager had arranged with industry people. These were the reasons on his calendar.

But Sutton was the reason beneath it.

Four days. That's all it had been since their last night at the cabin. Since she walked away with a half-smile that made him wonder what she was still keeping close.

His phone lit up as he set the empty coffee aside. It was his manager, efficient as ever.

Confirming our meetings this week. Let me know if anything shifts.

Wesley typed a brief response, though his eyes stayed on the skyline. Yellow cabs crawled along the arteries of the city, tiny streaks of color in the gray.

The last time cameras had charted his relationship, with Juliet, the interviews and the staged candids, everything real had been stripped away. It stopped being two people who loved each other and became content.

With Sutton, he didn't want content.

He wanted the unseen moments. Her socks on his couch. Her hair piled messily on top of her head. Her drawings smudged on paper. Her guard down. His too.

The plane dipped lower; his ears popped. His reflection wavered in the glass, familiar features he'd watched through other people's lenses for too many years.

The wheels touched down with a soft shudder. Sirens, ground equipment, and the restless pulse of a city waking seeped through the cabin walls.

He didn't know exactly where this leap would lead. He knew only one thing as the jet taxied toward the hangar:

She was worth the uncertainty.

***

Sutton sat curled in the corner of her couch, a blanket over her legs and a spread of artist submissions scattered across the coffee table. Her pencil tapped against her lower lip as she studied an abstract skyline, lightly sketching.

The buzzer jolted her out of her thoughts.

Her heart kicked.

She set the portfolio aside and pressed the intercom.

"Come on up," she said, already watching the end of the hallway, willing the elevator to move faster.

Seconds stretched.

Then the doors slid open, and Wesley stepped into view. Windswept hair, scarf loose around his neck, a takeout bag hanging from one hand.

She moved without thinking, crossing the hall and pressing herself into his arms.

"Hey," he murmured into her hair, voice rough from travel.

"I missed you," she whispered, fingers curling into his jacket.

He drew back just enough to lift the crumpled bag between them with a sheepish smile.

"I brought dinner. It's probably cold by now."

She laughed, still holding on. "I don't care about the food. I'm just glad you're here."

"We're here," he said simply, brushing a soft kiss over her lips. "That's what matters."

Inside, he looked around her apartment with an easy, appreciative sweep of his gaze: the books stacked in neat but lived-in piles, warm lamplight, framed art on the walls.

"So this is your place." His smile deepened. "It's very you. Clean, pulled together, but cozy."

"I'll take that as a compliment," she said.

"It is. Definitely."

They unpacked the containers in the kitchen, moving around each other with surprising ease.

Wesley set the bags aside and stepped closer, his hand settling at her waist.

"I wasn't sure if you'd really come," she admitted, voice softer than she meant.

He traced a slow line on her hip. "What, you thought I'd change my mind in four days?"

"Not change it," she said, looking up. "But I know your life. I wouldn't have blamed you if things pulled you away."

He lifted her chin gently.

"I meant what I said at the cabin. I want to be here. With you. This wasn't a holiday impulse. You've been on my mind nonstop."

Emotion tightened her throat. "You make it sound simple."

"It is," he said quietly. "For me."

He kissed her again, deeper. She slid her hands along his shoulders.

Wesley lifted her onto the counter, the cold marble startling for only a moment before his body replaced every distraction.

His thumb stroked the inside of her wrist, slowly and deliberately. Her pulse jumped and her hands tugged him closer.

His lips found hers again, then traced a path to the sensitive spot below her ear. Each kiss sent shivers down her spine. His hands slid under her shirt, thumbs brushing against her bra. Sutton arched into him, her breath catching as his mouth followed.

"You're going to be the death of me," Wesley murmured, his voice rough as his hands rested on her thighs. "But I don't care."

Sutton laughed softly.

"You're one to talk."

His hands slid up her thighs, pulling her against him. The contrast between the cold counter and the heat building between them heightened every sensation.

"Four days," she breathed against his lips. "Felt like a lifetime."

Wesley chuckled, his lips trailing along her jawline.

His hands claimed her thighs with deliberate pressure as he eliminated the space between them. Sutton's fingers found his jeans, working the buttons with growing boldness as each breathless catch fueled her confidence.

Wesley captured her wrists, his eyes darkening as a teasing smile played across his lips.

"Patience," he whispered against the sensitive hollow of her throat, his breath hot against her pulse.

Sutton arched an eyebrow, her mouth curving with mischief.

"That's rich, coming from you."

She rolled her hips against him, drawing a sharp inhale that made her skin tingle with power.

His laugh vibrated through the narrow space between them, intimate and rich with promise as he released her hands to trace the curve of her waist. Their bodies found a natural cadence together as he pushed inside of her, like waves meeting shore, inevitable and perfect.

She whispered his name like a prayer, feeling him respond with a tremor that coursed through them both.

Release came with a rush of warmth that cascaded through them both, drawing out a shared, shuddering breath. Wesley leaned forward until their foreheads touched, both catching their breath in the stillness.

Her fingers traced idle patterns along the damp skin of his neck while his hands remained at her waist, steady and possessive.

"Well," Sutton whispered, her voice honey-warm as a smile tugged at her lips. "That was one way to break in the kitchen counter."

Wesley's chest rumbled with quiet laughter as he lifted his gaze to hers.

"You think I'm done breaking it in?"

His thumb traced her lower lip, sending aftershocks of pleasure through her still-sensitive body.

Later, the apartment settled into a quiet rhythm. Half-eaten takeout containers crowded the coffee table. Sutton reclined against the cushions, her legs draped across Wesley's lap. He traced slow circles along her ankle, raising small goosebumps.

She stabbed a noodle. The sauce had long cooled, but the flavor still hit.

"Cold Thai isn't the worst thing, right?"

Wesley forked a bite from his carton.

"Could be worse. We could have had no Thai food at all."

"Spoken like a man who didn't come here for dinner," she said, nudging him.

He grinned.

"The food is definitely the side dish."

Her cheeks warmed despite her eye roll.

His gaze drifted to the pages beneath the containers: sketches, notes, color studies. He set his carton aside and lifted one.

"What's all this?"

Sutton sat up a little straighter.

"Something I'm working on. Or planning to."

"Tell me more."

"I want to host a showcase. Highlight local artists at a warehouse in March. I want it to feel intimate. Curated. Like stepping into a story instead of a room."

His eyes brightened.

"You're organizing it?"

"Curating it," she said with a small smile. "I've always loved art. I went to a gallery the other day and realized how much I missed creating something that's mine. It's something I've always wanted to do."

He studied her expression, thoughtful.

"It's exciting and terrifying. If it fails, it's on me. If it works, maybe it means there's more for me than planning other people's events."

"I think there is," he said simply.

She looked down at the sketches.

"You really think I can pull this off?"

"I know you can." His voice didn't waver. "You've been telling stories for other people for years. This is just the first time the story is yours."

"Also," he added lightly, "someone needs to taste-test the champagne and canapés. I'm willing to suffer."

She laughed, nudging him.

"So noble."

He kissed her forehead, lingering there.

"Whatever this becomes," he murmured, "I'm in your corner. Loudly or quietly. However, you need me."

She let the words sink in.

"Just knowing you believe in me, that's enough."

They talked until they completely forgot the takeout. Until the city blurred beyond the windows. He told her about his foundation and what he hoped to build. She described the story she wanted to tell through the art, and how she wanted people to feel the moment they stepped inside the showcase.

By the time they slipped into bed, the air between them held more than chemistry.

It held a real, imperfect, hopeful possibility.

Not a winter bubble. Not a pause.

They were building something, one deliberate choice at a time.

Twenty-Four

WEEKS EASED INTO A rhythm neither of them had expected, but both quietly cherished.

By day, Sutton navigated the chaos of event planning: client meetings, color swatches, crises disguised as "simple tweaks." Across the city, Wesley bounced between studio sessions, board calls for his foundation, and meetings that seemed to multiply the moment news spread he was staying in New York "for a while." The city tugged them in separate directions, each swallowed by their own responsibilities.

But the nights belonged entirely to them.

Some evenings, they ended up in his minimalist apartment, floor-to-ceiling windows framing the glittering skyline, the sleek furniture softened when Sutton curled onto the couch with her laptop and a glass of wine. On other nights, they met at her cozy place, where colorful throw pillows filled every corner with warmth. He always said her apartment felt like a home, while his felt like a very well-decorated layover.

Christmas pulled them apart, but New Year's Eve reunited them at a friend's SoHo loft. At midnight, while the room erupted in cheers and confetti, Wesley's fingers threaded through hers, his hand warm and steady at the small of her back. One grounding touch in a sea of celebration.

Two weeks later, Sutton stood in the produce aisle of her neighborhood market with her phone pressed to her ear, doing a quick round of grocery shopping.

"Eight weeks since you two met," Brynn declared, her voice crackling through Sutton's phone as Sutton dropped a Honeycrisp apple into her basket.

"Tell me about it," Sutton laughed, grabbing oat milk. "If someone had predicted this, I'd have laughed in their face."

"Well," Brynn said, sounding thoroughly smug, "you're welcome. Aren't you glad I invited him now?"

Sutton shook her head with a small laugh. "This trip didn't just change my plans. It rewrote everything."

"Complaining?" Brynn teased.

"Not even close." Sutton dodged a shopper with a scarf trailing behind her. "It's just strange. Stepping into something I didn't even know I wanted and now I can't imagine my life without it."

Brynn's voice softened. "You sound different when you talk about him. Lighter."

Sutton smiled right before Brynn sucked in a sharp breath.

"Oh God. Alexander just walked in. I need to..."

"Wait, Alexander's back?"

But the call had already disconnected.

Sutton tucked her phone into her coat pocket and headed to the cashier. Moments later she stepped into the December chill, wind sweeping across her cheeks in a biting rush.

The moment she opened her apartment door, a rich aroma wrapped around her: saffron, garlic, and citrus. Her stomach growled.

She dropped her keys and called out, "You're early!"

Wesley turned from the stove, wooden spoon lifted mid-stir, an apron tied crookedly around his waist. A streak of paprika dusted his forearm.

"Surprise," he said, smiling. "Paella's almost done."

He offered her the spoon. The flavor made her eyebrows shoot up.

"My favorite," she said softly. "You remembered."

"I pay attention." He leaned in and pressed a warm kiss to her forehead.

His key, her key, hung casually on their keychains now. A practical milestone, not ceremonial, but meaningful all the same.

"How was work?" he asked, setting out plates.

"The Gaga launch is intense," she said, unpacking groceries. "But the art showcase is coming together. I just need to confirm a few local artists. At least the warehouse is locked in."

Wesley looked up, steam curling around him.

"Well, I'm excited. Also, Sarah, Kyle, and Elliot. Everyone's excited."

Ever since they merged their lives a little more openly after the New Year's Eve party, a few of Wesley's closest confidants knew about them.

"That sounds great. This would be perfect for Kyle. Do you think he'd want to showcase any of his photography?" she asked, her shoulders relaxing.

He shrugged. "I don't know. I never asked." He smiled. "But I can. Either way, it's going to be incredible," he said as he plated the paella.

Sutton reached across the table, brushing his fingers.

"Having you there, especially behind the scenes for now, means everything."

His thumb traced her palm.

"Wherever you need me."

She took a bite, giving a small sound of approval.

"How was the studio?" she asked.

"Long day," he said, a small smile appearing, "but a good one."

These dinners were becoming a routine that felt effortless. Familiar. Like something rooted rather than rushed.

Wesley poured her wine, then lifted his glass toward hers.

"Here's to reinvention," he said, half teasing, half serious.

Later, they sank into their Friday ritual bath. Candlelight flickered against the tiled walls, turning the room into a golden cocoon.

Sutton leaned back against his chest, her head settling near his collarbone. His arms slipped around her waist beneath the warm water, fingertips tracing a slow pattern along her shoulder.

She lifted her glass, letting the cabernet warm her throat.

"I love these moments," she murmured.

"Me too," he said, voice low and steady. "This, us, this is the best part of my week. I didn't know normal could feel this special."

These evenings were their anchor, quiet, intimate, unhurried moments that grounded them in a world that could tilt sideways without warning.

Not dramatic.

Not flashy.

But theirs.

TWENTY-FIVE

THE SUNLIT STUDIO IN the Garment District hummed with soft, industrious energy. Leather scraps and spools of jewel-toned thread cluttered the wooden tables, while Sauvignon Blanc mingled with the earthy scent of fresh-cut hides. Conversations drifted in warm, creative murmurs as metal tools clinked and scissors snipped.

Sutton guided her scissors through a piece of caramel leather, each crisp cut falling into rhythm with her breath.

Beside her, Zoe leaned forward, her London accent lilting around a question she'd clearly been holding since they walked in.

"So," she whispered, a wicked glimmer in her eye, wine glass dangling from her fingertips, "you and Wesley, huh?"

The words hovered between them like floating stitches.

Sutton's hands paused before she resumed cutting with forced concentration. The smile tugged at her lips, betraying her.

"Yeah," she said softly. The single word carried more weight than she had intended. "I guess so."

Zoe's grin widened, her charming gap on full display. She lifted her glass in a mock toast.

"Girl, if it wasn't going to be me, I'm glad it's you."

She tapped her glass lightly against Sutton's.

"Now spill everything."

Across the room, a sewing machine whirred to life, its steady hum giving Sutton a few seconds to gather herself. She traced the smooth edge of the leather with her fingertips.

"Honestly, it just happened," she said quietly. "We talked, and suddenly everything made sense. I wasn't looking for it. But now..."

She exhaled.

"I can't imagine it any other way."

Zoe shook her head, curls bouncing.

"That's how it always is, isn't it? The quiet ones sneak up on you. Or the ugly ones with pleasant personalities."

"Oh, absolutely. Wesley's a real troll," Sutton said dryly, though warmth crept across her cheeks.

Their laughter bubbled over, loud enough that a silver-haired woman across the room peered at them over half-moon glasses. They ducked their heads like guilty schoolgirls, shoulders shaking with suppressed giggles.

When the laughter faded, Zoe's expression softened. The teasing slipped away.

"You're happy, right?" She asked, needle hovering above her leather.

Sutton met her gaze without flinching.

"Very."

The word landed softly, honest and sure.

"Happier than I've been in a long time."

Zoe nodded, satisfaction brightening her entire face.

"Good. That's all anyone wants for their friends."

She pushed her needle through the leather.

"But damn, between Graham and now Wesley, you've got to stop snatching up all the eligible men. Leave some crumbs for the rest of us."

Sutton laughed, the sound echoing lightly against the exposed brick.

Zoe tipped her head, her grin sharpening with curiosity.

"Speaking of, does that mean Graham's single now?"

The question hit harder than expected.

Sutton's fingers stilled on the cool leather. For a moment, the studio's chatter blurred into background noise. Something flickered inside her, but her heart stayed steady.

"I guess so," she said, her casual tone nearly convincing.

"Why are you interested?"

Zoe barked a laugh, nearly sloshing wine onto her half-stitched project.

"Nah. You two couldn't make it work in the same city, so there's no way we'd stand a chance across continents."

Her wink was playful; her eyes kind.

Relief slid through Sutton. Not because Zoe wasn't interested, but because the idea of Graham with someone she knew still pulled at something she'd rather ignore.

The instructor drifted over, murmuring praise as she traced a finger along Sutton's neatly aligned stitches.

"Beautiful work," she said before moving on.

Sutton lifted her bag, admiring the clean seams. Zoe held up her own crooked creation with a dramatic flourish.

"I think I missed my calling as a handbag designer," she declared.

"I'll send your portfolio to Vogue immediately," Sutton said solemnly.

"Damn right you will."

Zoe cackled, warm and unrestrained.

Two hours later, they stepped onto the busy sidewalk, their new leather bags swinging from their wrists. Afternoon sun drenched the street in honey-gold light. Car horns blared, food carts sizzled, and the city breathed around them.

Sutton inhaled deeply. A mix of summer warmth, street food, and the faint echo of wine clinging to her sweater.

Something inside her felt lighter. Steadier.

Sharing Wesley with someone from her old world diminished nothing. If anything, it made what she had feel more real. Less fragile. Less like a holiday fling and more like life.

Her bag bumped gently against her hip as she walked, the weight grounding her.

For the first time in a long time, she realized she wasn't holding her breath anymore.

Twenty-Six

Sutton and Wesley slipped into Garfunkel's, a speakeasy hidden behind a nondescript door you'd miss in a blink unless you knew exactly where to look. Copper-tinted light pooled across mahogany tables while saxophone notes floated through the air like smoke, wrapping around hushed conversations. Ice clinked against crystal, punctuating the room's rhythm.

Wesley's palm rested against the small of Sutton's back, warm through the silk of her dress as they followed the host to a secluded booth. His shoulders visibly dropped once they settled into the leather seats, the outside world dissolving at the threshold.

Applause rippled through the room as the saxophonist finished, and a hush fell. A single spotlight lit the stage. A singer stepped forward, her silver dress catching every glimmer of light. Her hair was artfully disheveled, a contrast to the stillness in her expression. She curled her fingers around the microphone stand

and closed her eyes. Her first note slipped out, barely louder than breath, yet Sutton felt it deep in her ribs.

This wasn't jazz from a speaker.

This was alive.

She glanced at Wesley beside her. His eyes followed the performance with the reverence of one artist witnessing another's craft.

Songs unfurled like velvet. Their charcuterie board slowly emptied between shared glances and whispered comments. The conversation that blooms only between songs.

Sutton traced the rim of her wineglass, drawing a crystalline note that shimmered between them.

"This is perfect," she murmured.

Wesley's smile curved, soft, and knowing.

"I'm glad. Whenever I'm in the city, this is my sanctuary. Jazz was the soundtrack of my childhood. I never inherited the voice, but the appreciation? That stuck."

***

They stepped onto rain-polished streets where lamplight fractured across puddles like shattered glass. Sutton tugged her coat tighter, January's bite creeping through the wool. Their breaths mingled in soft clouds as Wesley laced his fingers with hers.

"I love the city after rain," she said. "It's like it just took a deep breath."

He squeezed her hand.

"Or maybe it's holding one for us."

The first flash came like lightning. Sharp. Blinding.

Sutton recoiled. Another flash. Then another.

The quiet street erupted with voices, bodies, and the whir of cameras slicing through the air.

"Wesley! Look this way!"

"Who's the girl?"

"Is this your new girlfriend?"

Wesley's hand slipped from hers as he stepped forward, shoulders squared, jaw set.

"Back up," he barked. "My friend and I are just trying to leave."

Friend.

The word collided with her chest.

"Can we get a photo of the two of you together?"

His public distancing made sense. She knew that. She understood it.

But hearing it aloud, with cameras pointed at her like she was a curiosity, hollowed something inside her.

Sutton froze, breath catching. The memories of the last nine weeks flooded her: late-night dinners, quiet mornings in bed, whispered secrets shared in the dim light of the city. Now, the moments that had been private and sacred felt exposed, as if strangers could read them after someone had ripped open a diary and scattered its pages.

Wesley flagged a taxi with sharp urgency. With his arm braced in front of her as he guided her inside, the door slammed shut and muted the barrage outside.

The cab smelled of cheap citrus and stale air. Vinyl squeaked beneath them as the city streaked past in smeared ribbons of light.

Wesley reached for her hand.

Her fingers didn't tighten back.

"I never thought they'd find us there," he said, frustration roughening his voice. "That spot's usually safe."

Sutton turned from the window, throat tight.

"I always knew it was a possibility," she whispered. "I just didn't expect the reality to feel like this."

In his apartment, the tension never fully lifted. Wesley paced with his phone to his ear, speaking with Jen, his publicist. His voice was clipped and controlled. Sutton sat curled on the edge of the couch, her reflection faint in the floor-to-ceiling windows.

When he finally hung up, he crossed the room and knelt in front of her, taking her hands in his.

They were still cold.

Jen's on it," he mumbled. "We'll get ahead of this."

Sutton swallowed, tongue brushing a raw spot inside her cheek.

"I'm still anonymous. At least right now. That counts for something?"

Wesley hesitated. The faintest flinch.

"Tonight, yeah," he admitted. "But tomorrow... it's always different."

The truth settled between them, heavy and unavoidable.

He sat beside her, the couch creaking beneath him.

"This isn't how I wanted the world to meet us," he said. "But I swear, we can navigate this together. Whatever happens, what we've built doesn't belong to them."

He reached for her hand again.

Sutton blinked hard, refusing the sting behind her eyes.

She wasn't ready to let go.

Not even close.

But for the first time, she saw the steepness of the climb.

Twenty-Seven

Sutton lay motionless in Wesley's bed the next morning, tracing invisible patterns on the ceiling. Winter sunlight filtered through half-drawn curtains, painting the walls in strips of gold and gray. Her chest felt tight, each breath carrying the weight of unanswered questions.

Could she do this?

Could she survive in Wesley's fishbowl existence, where strangers would dissect her life, her choices, and her worth without ever knowing her at all?

She'd spent years building her life brick by brick, shaping a career and independence that felt sacred. The thought of sacrificing any part of that made her stomach knot. Yet the idea of walking away from him felt like slicing through something vital, an artery she wasn't sure she could live without.

In the living room, Wesley hunched over his laptop, jaw tight, shoulders locked. The headlines glared back at him in neon tabloid fonts:

"WESLEY & MYSTERY WOMAN SPOTTED IN NYC"

"POST-JULIET ROMANCE? WESLEY'S NEW LEADING LADY"

"WHO IS THE WOMAN STEALING WESLEY'S HEART?"

He clicked through them until the words blurred. Sutton, private, grounded, self-made, had disappeared the moment those camera flashes went off. He'd dragged her into his world without asking, and now the circus had swallowed her whole.

A thick knot of helplessness settled in his chest.

He'd survived this scrutiny for years. He knew where to duck, when to disappear, how to keep the world from touching the parts of himself he treasured. But Sutton, Sutton had no such armor.

Sutton stood in the doorway, framed by morning light. She looked pale, dark crescents pooling beneath her eyes, but there was something steady in the set of her shoulders.

He shut the laptop and crossed the room in three strides. Without speaking, she stepped into his arms, as though the space between them was carved for that purpose. Wesley's arms wrapped around her instantly, one hand sliding into her sleep-mussed hair, the other splayed between her shoulder blades.

Her cheek pressed against his chest, heartbeat against heartbeat. He lowered his lips to her temple, breathing in the faint trace of his shampoo in her hair.

They stayed like that, silent, anchored, their bodies saying what their words couldn't yet hold.

At last, Sutton whispered into the cotton of his shirt, "So... what's our plan?"

The word hit him like a pulse.

Our.

She wasn't retreating.

She wasn't blaming anyone.

She wasn't unraveling.

She was asking how *together* they would weather the storm.

***

By Saturday, the restlessness had hardened into something heavier. Hiding made the world feel smaller, like the walls were inching inward. After a blunt, no-sugar-coating call with Jen, their options were painfully clear:

Hide.

Live freely but invisibly.

Or face it head-on.

That morning, sunlight spilled across the rumpled sheets as Sutton rolled toward him, something bright flickering behind her eyes.

"Let's do brunch," she announced.

Wesley, propping himself on one elbow, stretched languidly as cotton sheets pooled at his waist.

"Sure, I can make something here."

She touched his forearm.

"No. I mean out. In public."

He blinked.

"Public?"

"Buvette," she said, the glint in her eyes equal parts dare and declaration.

His eyebrows shot up.

"You want to go to Buvette?"

She nodded, a slow smile curving at the edges.

"Yes, I'm tired of hiding. Let them talk. Let them speculate. We don't owe them anything. One day at a time, remember?"

He searched her face for doubt. When he found none, something eased in his chest. He leaned in and kissed her, a soft press that deepened as her fingers threaded through his hair.

"You," he murmured against her lips, "are incredible."

Buvette buzzed with Saturday life. Espresso machines hissed, silverware tapped against porcelain, and conversations folded into one. Wesley kept his cap low. Sutton wrapped her coat tight, though it was less about hiding and more about bracing.

They slid into a small corner table, knees touching beneath the battered wood. Steam curled from their cups, cutting through the scent of warm pastries.

"How are you feeling?" Wesley asked quietly.

Sutton lifted her cappuccino.

"I'm okay," she said, the words at odds with the knot twisting her stomach.

Wesley pivoted gently.

"How's the art exhibit coming along?"

Her face lit up like the sunrise.

"It's coming together. Local artists confirmed. I'm excited."

He couldn't stop the smile that spread across his face.

"I'm proud of you. Really proud."

Her shoulders loosened, breath easing out.

But the café, for all its comfort, wasn't forgiving.

Sidelong glances.

Whispers behind raised mugs.

Phones angled with fake subtlety.

Every stare pricked Sutton's skin.

By the time they finished, her pulse vibrated beneath her skin like a trapped bird.

They stepped outside; the cold sliced through the tension.

"Let's walk," Wesley said, and she nodded, grateful for the fresh air.

Cobblestone streets echoed under their steps, a rhythm both soothing and fragile. Sutton paused outside a small bookstore, its windows fogged, golden light spilling from within. Inside, books stood in neat stacks, spines of different colors creating a literary mosaic.

"I used to love places like this," she murmured. "Just getting lost."

A gust of wind swept down the street, whipping strands of her hair across her face.

Then something on her face shifted, quiet but unmistakable. The simple joy she'd once taken for granted now felt stolen.

Wesley touched her hand lightly.

"Let's go in."

Her fingers twisted the fringe of her scarf; her reflection fractured in the window.

"Maybe another time."

Beneath her calm exterior, doubt surged like a rising tide. Quickly and harshly. The bookstore window reflected two versions of herself: who she was and who she was becoming, and the chasm between them widened with each passing second.

"Hey," he said softly. "You okay?"

She nodded too quickly, her lips curving upward while her gaze remained distant.

"Yeah. I'm fine."

But the lie tasted metallic on her tongue.

She exhaled sharply.

"Actually, do you mind if I head home? I need to catch up on work."

The distance in her eyes hollowed something inside him.

Wesley swallowed.

"Sure. Whatever you need."

They hailed a taxi in brittle silence. The yellow car stopped with a puff of exhaust.

He held the door open.

"Call me later?"

"Yeah. Of course," she said, her voice quiet, polite, evasive. She slipped inside without meeting his eyes.

He remained on the sidewalk long after the cab disappeared into traffic, her absence settling heavily beside him.

The cold stung his lungs. He flexed his fingers, as if trying to grasp something that had already slipped.

Their morning had started with unity.

Defiance.

A team.

But now, standing alone on a winter street, Wesley felt something he hadn't felt since Juliet.

A crack. Hairline, but real.

And getting wider.

Twenty-Eight

Wesley stared at his blank phone screen, the darkness reflecting his hollow expression. No message. No missed calls. Five hours since Sutton had walked away, her shoulders rigid with unspoken thoughts. Time crawled forward in excruciating increments, each second gnawing at the edges of his sanity.

His footsteps echoed against the hardwood as he paced. The living room walls seemed to press inward with each turn, the silence broken only by his measured breathing and the occasional creak of the floorboards. The weight of his phone grew heavier with each check, the emptiness of the screen more accusatory.

Was she rethinking everything? Was the reality of being with him too much? Could he even blame her if it was?

As he sank into the leather sofa, his gaze caught on his guitar. The polished wood gleamed under the soft lamplight, beckoning. The instrument felt like an old friend in his hands, familiar curves settling against his body. His calloused fingertips found the strings, coaxing out notes that hung in the air like ghosts. Tonight, the music betrayed him, every chord carrying echoes of Sutton.

His phone vibrated against the coffee table, the sound electric in the quiet room. Wesley lunged for it, heart hammering against his ribs. The screen illuminated his face, hope crashing into disappointment as his manager's name flashed instead of hers.

"Damn it," he muttered, tossing the phone down. The thud reverberated through the room, making the silence that followed sharper, more complete.

He pressed his palms against his eyes until colors bloomed behind his lids, inhaling the scent of polish and wood from his guitar. His fingers hovered over the phone again, torn between respect and desperation. Every message he drafted evaporated unsent, the words inadequate against the weight of what he needed to say.

***

Sutton hunched over her desk, surrounded by a chaotic sprawl of art gallery notes that had overtaken every inch of the surface. Her laptop screen glowed, the email on it blurring as her focus drifted. The excitement that once fueled her project now felt as flat as day-old champagne.

Her phone lay just beyond her fingertips, screen dark, waiting. She'd promised to text Wesley, but her mind tangled around words that refused to form. The words she needed sat like stones in her throat, too heavy to lift.

The fear had crystallized as she'd watched strangers surreptitiously photograph him through the bookstore window, their whispers carrying to her ears despite their efforts to be discreet. The scene looped in her mind like a skipping record. Wesley was beside her on the sidewalk, her attention caught by the display window's orderly rows of spines and covers.

She remembered a time when books were just books, not potential backdrops for strangers' cameras. She saw her own reflection in the glass, standing beside him yet somehow separate; ordinary against his extraordinary fame. The realization had cut deep: this was her future with him. Always observed, just existing.

Sutton exhaled shakily, pushing the phone away. Not yet.

She ordered dinner from the Thai place down the block, its pad thai and spring rolls a familiar comfort. James Taylor's voice filled the apartment, the gentle guitar strumming a balm to her frayed nerves.

In the kitchen, the cork from her Roederer Estate Brut popped with a satisfying sound. The champagne fizzed into her glass, pale gold and effervescent. She took a sip, the crisp, yeasty notes dancing on her tongue; not flashy but complex, much like herself.

The comparison brought a sad smile to her lips just as the door buzzer cut through Taylor's melodies.

"Come up," she called into the intercom, expecting delivery.

When she opened the door, Wesley stood in the hallway, shoulders slightly hunched against the evening chill. His hair was windswept, cheeks flushed from the cold. Something raw and unguarded lingered in his gaze, stripping away his usual confidence.

"Hi," he said, the word barely audible.

"You're not the dinner I ordered," she replied, her attempt at levity falling flat.

They stood in her entryway; the silence stretched taut between them.

Wesley nodded toward the music floating through the apartment as he eventually walked inside.

"James Taylor, huh?" He hummed a few notes of *Fire and Rain,* his voice rough at the edges.

Sutton's smile didn't reach her eyes as she led him to the living room.

He perched on the sofa arm, fingers drumming against his thigh.

"You didn't call," he said finally.

No accusations, just hurt that made her chest tighten.

"I know."

Her voice was small, nearly lost in the space between them.

"I didn't know what to say."

"Say anything," Wesley urged, extending his hand. It was an offering, a lifeline. "Please don't shut me out."

Sutton stared at his outstretched hand, at the calluses on his fingertips from years of guitar strings. That hand had traced the curve of her spine, had held hers through crowded streets, had created music that moved thousands.

It represented everything beautiful and terrifying about what they'd built.

"Please," he whispered, the word cracking with emotion.

The doorbell's shrill interruption made them both flinch.

"My dinner," she murmured, relief and frustration mingling as she moved to answer.

Wesley remained in the living room, shoulders tight with tension.

When Sutton returned, she set the paper bag on the kitchen counter, the smell of spices and herbs filling the air. She braced her hands against the edge, knuckles whitening as Taylor's *Secret O' Life* wove through the apartment.

When she turned, something had shifted in her expression, a clarity that hadn't been there before.

Wesley stood, recognizing the change.

This time, when he reached out, she moved toward him without hesitation.

Her fingers slid between his. The distance between them disappeared as she pressed her lips to his, the kiss carrying the force of everything unsaid.

It tasted of champagne and desperation, of fear and longing.

Wesley's arms encircled her. His heart hammered against hers as the kiss deepened, his hands splayed across her back, drawing her closer until the heat between them was almost unbearable.

Every touch carried the weight of their unspoken fears, a physical reminder of what bound them together.

Sutton's fingers fumbled with his waistband as he lifted her shirt over her head, the fabric pooling at their feet. He lifted her with ease, her legs wrapping around his waist, the friction between them electric.

They barely made it to the hallway, her back meeting the cool wall as their bodies found a desperate rhythm. The contrast of the cold surface against her heated skin sent shivers down her spine, intensifying every sensation as they moved together.

When stillness finally settled over them, Sutton pressed her forehead against his, their breaths mingling in the narrow space between.

Her voice trembled, barely audible even in the quiet.

"I love you..."

The words hung in the air, precious and fragile.

"But it's ruining me."

Twenty-Nine

Morning light filtered through the curtains, painting the bedroom in muted gold. Sutton's fingers trailed along cool, empty sheets, a tangible reminder of Wesley's absence. Two weeks since they'd ended, and still each morning greeted her with the same hollow silence. The air felt heavier somehow, as if the walls themselves missed his presence.

At her desk, project files sprawled in organized chaos amid the persistent ping of notifications. Sutton moved through her tasks with mechanical precision; her surface calm betrayed only by the slight tremor in her hands. Colleagues passed her with soft smiles and gentle nods, their eyes holding questions they wouldn't ask. Their silent support both comforted and underscored how far from normal her world had tilted.

The downtown lounge buzzed with evening conversation, its amber lighting casting protective shadows over their corner booth. Sutton breathed in the rich scent of seared garlic and wine, letting the cozy atmosphere settle around her as Brynn slid into the seat across from her.

Brynn's gaze traveled over Sutton's face, lingering on the shadows beneath her eyes.

"You look good," she said, wine glass poised at her lips. "All things considered."

Sutton attempted a smile.

"Work keeps me busy." The words fell between them, soft and brittle. "But when everything slows down..." Her voice faded to a whisper that barely carried above the restaurant's ambient noise.

The candlelight carved shadows beneath Brynn's eyes as she leaned closer, her forehead creased with worry.

"Have you heard from him?"

Sutton shook her head.

"No." The slight crack in her voice betrayed her composed exterior. "It's complicated. Everything happened so fast, and then..." She swallowed hard.

"Have you talked to him?" she asked.

When Brynn shook her head, something inside Sutton deflated. She'd been grasping for even the smallest connection to Wesley, some evidence he still existed in their shared world. She took a breath and looked out the window, where streetlights smeared into golden halos through the glass.

"I thought I could handle it," she said finally, her voice barely audible above the restaurant's ambient chatter. "But the reality was strangers tracking your movements, camera flashes ambushing you, whispers that followed you everywhere. It's like drowning in plain sight."

She sipped her wine, wincing as the once-sweet merlot turned sharp on her tongue.

"I love him. I do. But I don't know if I belong in his life."

Brynn's eyebrows arched, the admission hanging between them like suspended crystal.

"Did you tell him that?"

Sutton's forehead creased.

"What? Did I tell him what?"

"That you love him?"

Sutton nodded, twisting her napkin between restless fingers. The overhead lights caught the moisture gathering in her eyes.

Brynn leaned forward, the ice in her new cocktail clinking softly as she went to pick it up.

"How did he respond?"

A pained smile flickered across Sutton's face, her shoulders hunching slightly as if bracing for impact.

"Well, I said it. I told him I loved him, but I also said too much."

"What do you mean?" Brynn asked, confused.

Sutton looked down, embarrassed. "I told him that loving him was ruining me."

A hollow laugh slipped out of her, brittle as thin ice. Her fingers traced the condensation on her glass, leaving parallel trails like tear tracks.

"Yikes," Brynn murmured, raising her cocktail to her lips, taking a measured sip.

"Yeah, it wasn't my finest moment." Sutton's voice dropped to a whisper. "But it is true in a way. Loving him is hard. Loving him is turning my life upside down."

Brynn nodded, the soft clink of her bracelets punctuating the silence between them.

"Maybe it's not ruining me. I don't really know what I meant by that, to be honest. And it was hurtful for him to hear. I shouldn't have said it, but there was no coming back from it."

Brynn's brow furrowed, the tiny lines deepening around her eyes.

"Sutton, you've built your life on your terms. You're one of the most grounded people I know. If Wesley's the person who makes you happy, you'll find a way. But it has to work for you, too."

Sutton stared into the deep crimson of her wine.

"That kind of pressure isn't fair to anyone."

Brynn's voice carried a firmness that cut through Sutton's fog.

"But you have to ask yourself this: is he worth it? If he is, maybe it's worth the fight."

"I wanted to make it work with him," Sutton whispered, tracing the rim of her glass. "But every step closer to his world felt like a step away from mine."

Brynn reached across the table, her warm palm covering Sutton's trembling fingers.

"Listen to me. With or without Wesley, you're still Sutton. That doesn't change, even when everything else does."

***

The warehouse smelled of paint, sawdust, and possibility.

"So?" Maya spread her arms wide as Sutton stepped into the open space, winter light streaming through tall windows. "You still see it?"

Sutton turned in a slow circle, her boots echoing across the concrete floor. Bare brick. Exposed beams.

She didn't just see it; she felt it.

In her mind, the art space transformed. Soft pools of light illuminated each canvas. Murmurs of conversation roamed the room like a slow tide. Glassware chimed softly against trays. A string quartet tucked into the corner, weaving through the hush.

Not Valentina's vision. Hers.

Maya grinned.

"Good. We've got a few weeks until the art showcase. Floor plan's due Friday. Lighting test next week. I'll email you the mockups tonight."

"Perfect," Sutton said, her chest expanding with something that felt suspiciously like joy.

As she walked through the space, fingertips grazing the cold brick, she could almost hear the voice that kept her grounded on nights when anxiety threatened to unravel her.

You should start again. I'd love to see the world through your perspective.

Wesley's words from months ago drifted through her memory. She let them land, then gently set them aside.

"Okay." Sutton squared her shoulders, turning back to Maya. "Let's talk lighting zones and sightlines."

Thirty

Wesley sat in a glass-walled conference room suspended above Los Angeles, the city sprawling beneath him like a glittering circuit board. Around the table: Jen, his publicist, her nails tapping an impatient rhythm against her tablet; Kevin, his manager, posture unyielding; Brandon, his producer, fingers drumming; and the label executives with polished watches and curated smiles.

"The single will generate immediate buzz," Jen said, crisp and confident. "When are we targeting an album release?"

Brandon straightened.

"We're completing the last track. Fourteen, maybe sixteen songs total."

Kevin picked up with the press tour, outlining the rollout of interviews, appearances, and future tour dates. His voice faded into background noise as another echoed louder in Wesley's mind.

I love you. But it's ruining me.

The memory cut clean through the corporate noise.

"Wesley?" Jen's voice snapped him back.

He blinked, refocusing.

"Sorry, what?"

Jen's expression softened.

"Maybe we table this for now. Pick up later in the week."

He nodded, already standing. Relief hit like air after a long dive.

Outside, the city pulsed, but it all sounded muted, underwater. He slid on his sunglasses, sank into the leather of the SUV, and shut the world out with a quiet click.

At home, silence greeted him like a familiar ache. The stillness pressed in, heavy as humidity. For days, he'd hidden in the studio, but every chord felt hollow; every lyric circled the same gravity well. Creativity had once saved him. Now, it only mirrored his loss.

He turned instead to the gym: the bite of iron, the sting of sweat, the effort that left no room for thought. For a while, that helped, until memory pushed its way in again.

***

Two Weeks Earlier

Sutton's back hit the hallway wall, her breath still shallow. His shirt hung open, the air between them charged with the aftershock of what had just happened. Their hearts hadn't caught up with their bodies yet.

He leaned against the opposite wall, chest rising and falling, trying to steady himself. For a few long seconds, neither spoke. The silence was deafening.

Wesley blinked, every muscle in his body going still.

"You love me, but it's ruining you?"

His tone was quiet, but the disbelief beneath it was sharp enough to cut.

"I shouldn't have said it like that," she blurted. "I just feel like I'm drowning."

He wanted to tell her she was wrong, that love should've been enough, but the truth was already between them. His life was overwhelming, even for him. The noise, the expectations, the constant eyes. How could he expect her to bear it too?

"Sutton," he said, "I'm more than the fame, more than the chaos. My life can be overwhelming; I know that. When I pulled away from it all, I found a way to breathe again. I faced my demons and rebuilt myself, piece by piece. When you came into my life, I may have been in a better place, but I still struggle. This... us... It's not easy for me either."

Sutton shifted closer, her hand hovering near his before her fingers lightly caught the edge of his sleeve. He stilled.

"This scares me too," he confessed, the words raw in his throat. "Stepping back into that world terrifies me. I don't want to lose myself again. But I don't want to lose you either. I'm still figuring out how to balance it all."

She took a shaky breath.

"I don't want to lose you. But I also don't know how to fight to exist inside your life."

He stepped toward her slowly, stopping close enough that the space between them felt fragile.

"You think walking away will hurt less?"

Her eyes filled again.

"No. But staying might destroy me."

His next words felt like a betrayal, even as they carried undeniable truth.

"If we can't find a way to bridge our worlds," he said, voice rough, "then maybe love isn't the anchor we hoped it was."

The words landed between them, sharp and final.

Sutton closed the last inch of space, her hands unsteady as they gathered in the fabric of his shirt.

"I want it to be enough," she said.

He held her tightly, his arms encircling her like a life raft. He searched for words to fix what was breaking, to convince them both they could weather this storm. But the truth settled between them, immovable as stone.

Sutton pulled back slightly, her hands lingering on his chest, the warmth of her palms seeping through his shirt. Her eyes reflected a love that recognized its boundaries.

"You deserve someone who can make peace with your world," she whispered, her voice steadier now despite the tears.

"Someone who can stand beside you without fear. I wanted to be that person. I really did."

She let out a soft, humorless scoff. "I thought I could."

Wesley's hands trembled as he cupped her face, his thumbs brushing away tears that clung to her skin.

She searched his eyes, looking for hope but finding only the reflection of her own pain.

"I hate this," she whispered, her voice fraying at the edges. "I hate that I love you, and it's still not enough."

"I hate it too," he admitted, the words rough as sandpaper.

Sutton pressed against him one last time, her cheek against his chest, her heartbeat a rapid flutter he could feel through his shirt. His arms tightened around her, muscles refusing to let go even as his mind accepted the inevitable. The scent of her hair, the warmth of her body, he tried to memorize it all.

"I should head back to my place tonight," he whispered. Each syllable felt like more of a heartbreak, but he knew it was the only truth left.

As he moved toward the door, each step felt heavier than the last. At the threshold, he paused, hand resting on the cool metal of the doorknob.

He turned back. Their eyes met one final time.

The pain in her gaze mirrored his own, raw and bottomless. No words remained; all had been spent. In that silent exchange, every hope, regret, and ounce of love lay exposed.

When the door clicked shut behind him, the sound reverberated through his bones, a period at the end of their story.

Pain stabbed through him, sharp and relentless, but beneath it lay clarity. As desperately as they had tried, they couldn't be what the other needed, not in the ways that truly mattered.

He couldn't blame her. She deserved to honor her fears, her needs, her life.

She had chosen herself, and deep down, he respected her for it.

Dammit, he loved her for it.

***

Present Day

In his home gym, the memory pounded louder than his heartbeat. His lungs burned with every breath. The dumbbells slipped from his grip, clattering to the floor that echoed through the empty room.

Wesley sank onto the bench, elbows braced against his thighs, face buried in his palms. Sweat stung his eyes.

The grief hit harder now than it had the night he'd left. The question gnawed at him: could it still be love if they hadn't fought harder for it, or worse, if it had never been enough to begin with?

The thought constricted his chest, heavier than any weight he'd ever lifted.

Was this what letting go felt like? The hollow ache of surrender. The carousel of what-ifs. The unbearable thought was that maybe they'd let go of something rare because holding on had become too painful.

For the first time in years, Wesley understood that some battles left no victors, only two people walking away, carrying wounds that would never fully heal.

Thirty-One

The crisp air carried notes of blooming tulips as Sutton wrapped her fingers around the ceramic mug, stealing its heat while the morning air nipped at her neck. Cobblestones gleamed with dew beneath cafe tables. Around her, the street moved in soft rhythm: footsteps on stone, snippets of conversation, a bicycle bell chiming somewhere down the block.

Her omelet sat half-eaten, steam long gone. The toast beside it had cooled, its butter firm. Sutton pressed her phone to her ear, Brynn's voice threading through like a current in choppy water.

"I swear, if Alexander doesn't stop rearranging my bookshelf every time he visits, we're going to have problems," Brynn said, equal parts irritation and affection.

Sutton smiled, nudging egg fragments across her plate with her fork.

"You could just give in to his alphabetizing obsession. It's not like you actually read those books."

"The audacity!" Brynn gasped. "I read some of them. Occasionally. When the stars align."

Their laughter softened, then faded into a quiet pause.

"So," Brynn said, her voice lower now. "What's really going on with you?"

Sutton's gaze drifted to the street, where trees stretched against a bright blue sky.

"The usual," she said. "I'm okay. Taking each day as it comes."

Brynn didn't answer right away. When she did, her tone was gentler.

"You're doing better than you think. Breakups aren't easy, but you're handling it."

A shadow fell across the table, cutting through the sunlight. Sutton looked up, startled. Marcus stood there, smiling easily, sunlight glinting off his watch. He pulled out the chair across from her, the scrape of metal on stone breaking the stillness.

"Morning, sunshine," he said, his voice warm.

Sutton blinked, her phone still pressed to her ear.

"Marcus?"

"Surprise!" Brynn's triumphant voice came through the receiver.

Realization washed over Sutton.

"You didn't."

"Oh, I did," Brynn said, clearly pleased with herself. "Someone has to pull you back to the land of the living, and since I'm in L.A., Marcus is the next best thing."

Sutton sighed, though a reluctant smile tugged at her lips. "Well played."

She ended the call and set the phone down. Marcus leaned back, looking smug.

"You can thank me later," he said, reaching across to steal her toast. The crunch of his bite filled the pause.

Sutton crossed her arms, eyes narrowing.

"Are you here to gloat?"

His grin softened.

"No. Just checking in. We don't choose who we fall for. I've been there too."

A waiter approached, and Marcus ordered coffee. The smell of freshly ground beans filled the air.

"Brynn says you've gone full hermit," he teased. "I had to make sure it didn't escalate to black veils and feeding pigeons in Central Park."

"I'm not avoiding people," Sutton said, pleating her napkin into tiny folds.

"Of course not. Cold eggs and staring into space are textbook signs of thriving."

Her laugh slipped out before she could stop it. Marcus smiled.

"See? You're still in there," he said. "You just need a distraction. Lucky for you, I'm good at that."

He launched into a story about a disastrous dinner party, his hands painting chaos in the air. Sutton laughed until her sides ached. The tension that had lived in her shoulders for weeks finally eased.

She smiled, recalling the night her power went out in the middle of a winter storm and he let her crash on his couch until it was restored. They'd spent the night trading stories, sharing takeout, and laughing over old memories until the first light crept through his blinds. That had always been Marcus: levity wrapped in loyalty.

"Thank you," she said when their laughter faded. Her voice was quiet but full of meaning.

Marcus's teasing softened into something more sincere.

"Anytime. You don't have to do all this alone. You've got people. Me, Brynn..." He grinned. "Probably Alexander if you bribe him with some superb wine."

Sutton shook her head, smiling.

"It's hard to let people in sometimes."

"Your friends don't quit easily," Marcus said, brushing crumbs from the table. "Brynn has her grand gestures. I prefer smaller ones."

Sunlight filtered through the budding trees,. The road ahead was still uncertain, but surrounded by spring's promise and the quiet steadiness of friendship, she let herself believe she might eventually find her way.

THIRTY-TWO

WEEKS MELTED OFF THE calendar before the night of Sutton's art exhibition finally arrived.

The gallery pulsed with life: crystal glasses clinking, perfume mingling with the faint tang of fresh paint, conversations swelling and fading in waves. Sutton moved through it all with practiced ease, silk brushing her skin, each compliment sewing another quiet stitch where she'd once felt torn.

Color exploded from every wall. Canvases shouted and whispered; sculptures reached toward the ceiling, catching light like breath. Sutton's hands still remembered the weight of each piece she'd placed, her vision finally alive in three dimensions.

Brynn's laugh carried across the room, bright and unfiltered. She stood near Marcus and Cassie, her joy wrapping around Sutton like something familiar. Still, between conversations, she glanced toward the door, and within her an ache bloomed in the hollow where Wesley's presence should have been.

Halfway through explaining a painter's technique, Sutton froze.

A figure had just stepped into the doorway. Her breath caught. For one dizzy heartbeat, the crowd blurred, and the air sharpened. He came.

She mumbled an apology to the patron and started moving, weaving through clusters of guests, pulse climbing. Each step brought the silhouette into focus: the jacket, the stance, the confident ease she'd memorized once upon a time.

But when he turned, it wasn't Wesley.

"Graham?"

The name slipped out on a breath.

He smiled, with the same grounded ease she hadn't realized she missed.

"Surprised?"

The rush of confusion and relief tangled in her chest.

"A little," she admitted, laughter catching on the edge of her words.

"Marcus mentioned it," he said. "I had to see it for myself." His gaze swept the room before finding her again. "It's incredible, Sutton."

She smiled, almost speechless. For a second, words seemed unnecessary.

They fell into conversation easily, laughter threading through the noise of the room as if no time had passed at all. Graham listened intently, asking about each piece, every artist.

His laughter drew her in until the noise of the crowd faded to a soft blur.

When one curator waved her over to answer a question about pricing, she excused herself with a quick smile and moved away.

Across the room, Brynn noticed.

A minute later, she drifted toward Graham, wineglass in hand, her bracelets catching the light.

"Well, well," she said, arching a brow. "Didn't expect to see you in an art gallery. Expanding your horizons?"

"Maybe," Graham said easily. "Or maybe I heard there'd be free wine and excellent company."

Brynn laughed, tipping her glass.

"Sure. Because that's all this is about." Her glance flicked toward Sutton, who was now surrounded by guests near the far wall. "And I thought you were here for a more... curated exhibit."

Something softened in Graham's expression.

"She makes the art world more captivating," he said quietly. "But I promise I'm on my best behavior."

Brynn studied him for a moment, her expression assessing before she gave a slow nod.

"You'd better be. The last thing Sutton needs is another complication walking through her door in designer shoes."

He raised his hands, palms forward.

"I'm not here to shake things up. I'm here to support, in a completely non-dramatic, art-appreciating way."

His voice dropped half an octave, shedding its lightness.

"Sutton deserves good things," he said quietly. "I'm not here to get in the way of that."

Brynn studied him, her gaze sharp as a curator's. The teasing edge softened, giving way to something more thoughtful.

"Alright," she said finally, a sigh slipping through her words. "Then let's enjoy the night and celebrate Sutton."

By the time Sutton returned, Brynn had already melted back into another conversation, leaving Graham with that familiar, unreadable smile.

And as the last guests drifted out and the lights dimmed to a honeyed glow, he was still there, waiting by a column.

"Sutton," he said, voice low. "You should be proud of yourself. This is all you."

"Thank you." She smiled, appreciative. "It means a lot that you came. It was unexpected, but in the best way."

He smiled, the confidence in it softened by patience.

"Coffee next week? Keep it simple."

The offer lingered between them. Sutton hesitated, then nodded.

"I'd like that."

He turned to leave, and she watched him disappear into the city streets.

Perhaps life didn't repeat the past, but it reminded her that some stories simply paused between chapters.

Thirty-Three

Spring had seized the city, painting the streets in wild color and soft light. At Maman, sunlight filtered through the striped awning, striping the outdoor tables where Sutton approached.

Graham was already there, smile familiar in that quietly disarming way she hadn't realized she'd missed.

"Hey," she said, her voice catching on something lighter than she expected.

He rose, jacket pulling clean across his shoulders as he wrapped her in a brief hug. His cashmere sleeve brushed her cheek, carrying the scent of cologne and memory. Around them, the clink of cups and soft laughter threaded through the cafe.

"I got your favorite," he said, sliding a flat white across the table. The foam curled into a perfect spiral.

"You remembered."

"Some things are hard to forget."

They fell into conversation easily. Her latest work became his questions; his new startup turned into her curiosity. Words overlapped, laughter spilling out before either of them tried to hold it back.

Sutton leaned forward, the scent of espresso and pastry wrapping around them.

"You went and did it," Graham said finally, his tone gentler. "The gallery opening, everything you described back then. I knew you would, but seeing it come to life? It's remarkable."

"You make it sound so simple," she said quietly. "It wasn't."

"Nothing worth having ever is." He hesitated. "But it's worth it, right? Even when it's messy."

Sutton met his gaze.

"Especially when it's messy."

The air between them changed subtly, charged.

When the café emptied, Graham suggested a walk, and Sutton was glad he did. She found herself enjoying his company in a way she hadn't expected.

They wound through streets where cherry blossoms drifted down like pale confetti.

"Do you ever think about how much has changed?" Graham asked as they passed a park where kids chased bubbles that burst midair in flashes of color.

"All the time," she said. "Sometimes I wonder whether it strengthened me, or if things are just different."

"And you?" she added.

He smiled.

"Absolutely. I used to chase the next thing without even knowing why. Now I'm learning to actually be here for what's in front of me."

He looked at her when he said it, and she felt the weight of it settle.

They found their way onto the High Line. The river breeze tugged at her hair; the air tasted faintly of salt and street food. He bought them falafel wraps, and they sat on a bench overlooking the Hudson.

"You seem different, too," he said after a while. "But in the kind of way that comes from knowing what matters."

"I'm still figuring it out," she said, smiling slightly. "But I'm closer."

His eyes didn't leave hers.

"You've always been closer than you think."

Silence lingered, comfortable, weighted with the pull of something almost rediscovered.

When they finally stood, neither hurried. The sun had dropped low, painting amber streaks across the water.

"I had a great time today," Graham said.

"Me too."

He brushed her elbow; his touch was unhurried.

"Dinner? Saturday?"

She nodded, her expression gentling.

"Dinner sounds perfect."

Sutton waited for the ghost of Wesley to rise, the reflex she could never quite shake.

But it didn't.

Only the echo of her own laughter remained, along with the quiet certainty that something had shifted.

Thirty-Four

"What do you mean?" Sutton's voice trailed as she paced her living room. Outside, Manhattan pulsed under the amber wash of evening. The city moved while she stood still.

"Don't play coy." Brynn's voice crackled through the speaker, half amusement, half challenge. "You know exactly what I mean. Spill it."

Sutton stopped at the window, watching the skyline blur through her reflection.

"I don't know, Brynn," she said finally. "I genuinely don't know what I'm doing."

"Bullshit." Brynn's laugh rang through the line, bright and sharp. "Do you want to be with him? Are you falling for Graham again?"

The question landed heavily. Sutton pressed her palm to the cool glass, the city a constellation beneath her hand.

“I don’t know,” she said again, quieter. “What do you want me to say? Yes, Graham still makes me laugh. Yes, when he rolled up his sleeves, I remembered what it felt like to have those arms around me.” She paused, voice thinning. “And yes, sometimes I wonder what would happen if I just let myself fall.”

Her breath clouded the window.

“But do I miss Wesley?” Her voice cracked. “Every. Single. Day.”

Silence filled the line.

When Brynn finally spoke, her tone softened.

“Sutton, you can’t do this, not to Graham or yourself. If there’s something real there, try. But don’t use him to patch what’s still bleeding.”

Sutton sank into the couch, the cushions exhaling beneath her.

“I know,” she whispered. “You’re right.”

But knowing didn’t make it easier.

***

Graham arrived at eight sharp on Saturday. Sutton smoothed her black dress, willing her heartbeat to settle before she opened the door.

Café Carmellini glowed softly under low lighting, the scent of truffle butter curling through the air. Jazz floated above the clink of glasses, just enough to fill the quiet.

Once seated, Sutton reached for the cocktail menu as if it could shield her from what she needed to say.

"So," Graham said when the waiter left. "Tell me about your week."

"It was good," she said, her smile practiced. "Valentina asked me to help with the Cartier Met Gala afterparty. It's a big deal."

"The Met Gala," he repeated, eyes warm. "That's incredible." He raised his glass. "To well-deserved recognition."

Their glasses touched with a soft chime. But Sutton's smile faltered, and Graham noticed.

"You're not excited?" he asked gently.

"I am," she blurted. "It's just that there is a lot on my mind."

"Outside of work?"

Her throat tightened.

"The part that involves my heart."

Graham stilled, gaze steady.

"Wesley?" he asked softly.

His name landed between them like static.

"Yes," she said. "How did you know?"

"Marcus," he said simply, then after a pause, "Do you want to talk about it?"

She exhaled, staring into her glass.

"We ended things more than a month ago. His life is complicated. It was the right choice. But that doesn't mean it didn't hurt."

Graham nodded, fingers drumming lightly against the tablecloth.

"I appreciate your honesty," he said. Then, quieter: "Do you still have feelings for him?"

The question hit something tender.

"I do," she admitted. "I wish I didn't, but I can't pretend it's gone."

He nodded once, slowly, absorbing the truth without flinching.

"That's not what I hoped to hear," he said, voice even. "But I've been there."

He traced the rim of his glass with one finger.

"Complicated doesn't scare me off, Sutton."

"Graham..." she started, the ache behind his patience tugging at her.

He shook his head, a faint smile tugging at his mouth.

"Two winters ago, I walked away when I shouldn't have. I'm not doing that again. You need time; I'll give it. You need space, I'll make it. Just—" He leaned forward, voice steady. "If I'm not it, don't let me linger."

His words struck deep.

"I don't want to hurt you," she whispered.

"Then don't," he said simply. "But if you're not ready, I can handle that too. I'm here because I want to be."

Her throat thickened.

"You're really all in this time."

"I am," he said.

She managed a small smile, fragile but real.

"Then let's see where it takes us."

His answering smile reached his eyes.

"To wherever it takes us."

After dinner, the city air was cool against her bare shoulders. Their hands brushed once, twice, before Graham's fingers finally threaded through hers.

At her building, the streetlight split his face into light and shadow, his gaze lingering on her like a touch.

"Despite our dinner conversation," he said, his voice dipping low, "I still consider myself fortunate."

"How so?" she asked, her smile curving despite herself.

"Because now I get the chance to recover what we lost."

Before she could answer, he drew her closer, one hand tracing the back of her neck in a slow, unhurried motion. His lips found hers in a feather-light kiss, then deepened, deliberate and steady, until the world narrowed to the space between them.

When he finally pulled back, his mouth brushed her ear, his whisper roughened by restraint.

"And I've always been good at making up for lost time."

Her pulse skipped, traitorous. Goosebumps chased across her skin, her knees softening against the pavement.

They lingered, close enough that the air between them pulsed with leftover heat. Then Graham eased back, a small, satisfied smile curving his lips.

"Goodnight, Sutton."

She managed barely.

"Goodnight."

Inside her apartment, Sutton pressed her back against the door, breath uneven. The taste of him lingered.

Her heart ached for the simplicity Graham offered, but she knew he deserved more than the fractured attention of someone still haunted by another name.

Their connection had always been magnetic, brief, unfinished. This time, she wanted it to hold, something that could last, something she could stand on without fear of collapse.

Still, as the city moved outside her window, another memory flickered quietly at the edges of her mind, a voice she wasn't ready to forget, a song that hadn't quite stopped playing.

Thirty-Five

Four and a half months stretched between Sutton and Wesley like a straight highway at dusk, no sharp turns or sudden drop-offs, just an endless stretch of distance neither of them seemed ready to cross.

Spring's cherry blossoms inched open and fell again. Summer heat began to shimmer on the concrete. They moved through their lives with practiced purpose, each of them convincing the world, and mostly themselves, that they were fine.

Wesley tugged his headphones down to rest around his neck, sweat cooling at the nape of his neck as he leaned against the sound booth wall. The track for *Sacrifice* circled back to the bridge, that same sixteen bars they'd looped half a dozen times today.

"Take it from the top of the bridge again," came the producer's voice through the speakers. "You've almost got it, man. Just don't hold back."

Easy for him to say.

Wesley closed his eyes, fingers flexing around the mic stand. His pulse thudded in his ears, louder than the faint click track bleeding through the glass from the control room.

In the end, it's not the fame,

Not a crowd that knows my name.

He sang, letting the words scrape raw on the way out. On the other side of the glass, the producer's face softened, then went still, listening.

When the take ended, silence filled the booth. That strange, padded silence where you hear your own breathing, your own doubts.

The intercom crackled.

"That was it," the producer said quietly. "Come in and listen."

Wesley set the headphones down and stepped out. The hallway smelled faintly of old coffee and dust, a familiar mix that once felt like home. Now, it just smelled like work.

Kevin was perched on the arm of the studio couch, tablet in hand, tour calendar glowing on the screen. His gaze flicked between the dates and Wesley's face.

"Listen to this first," the producer said, tapping the keyboard.

The bridge poured through the speakers; the studio filled with the sound of his own voice. It was rougher now, lived in. Less polished than the label usually liked.

Wesley folded his arms, feeling the lyrics press against his ribs as if someone had written them on the inside of his skin.

"That's the one," the producer said when it finished. "Whatever you pulled from? That was real."

"Yeah," Wesley murmured. "It was."

Kevin let the moment breathe before clearing his throat.

"The label's buzzing. Pre-saves are through the roof," he said, pushing the tablet toward Wesley. "They think *Sacrifice*'s going to be the anchor of the tour. They're already calling this your comeback era."

"Didn't know I'd left," Wesley said lightly, but the joke fell flat.

"Look," Kevin said, tapping a date in late summer, circling it idly. "You're doing the work. You're showing up sober, on time, in tune. I'm proud of you. The label's obsessed with you. But I want to make sure you don't disappear in the middle of your own comeback."

"I'm not disappearing," Wesley said, a reflex bristle.

The tension eased, but didn't fully break. When Kevin left, tablet tucked under his arm, the studio felt too big, the quiet after the door closed pressing heavy against Wesley's chest.

The track for *Sacrifice* played softly through the control room speakers, bleeding under the door. The bridge hit like it always did.

It's the touch of your hand,

The way you understand.

He leaned his head back against the wall, eyes closed, letting the lyrics wash over him.

He didn't miss Sutton in a way that fit neatly into songs. Not exactly. He missed the version of himself who let her see him. The one who'd imagined a life made up of small, quiet days and Friday night dinners instead of hotel carpets and neon.

By the time the sun dropped, he'd shaken it off enough to head home. He had another session tomorrow. Another meeting. Another city to agree to.

***

Sutton walked into the Cartier Met Gala afterparty. The chandeliers she had negotiated for an entire month blazed overhead, turning the room into a constellation she'd built with her own hands.

Diamonds scattered light across mirrored walls, champagne flutes clinked with practiced cheer, and models drifted through the room in gowns worth more than Sutton's annual rent. Valentina had signed off on every floral arrangement. Every chair angle matched the CAD drawings Sutton had agonized over.

"You did it again," Mark murmured at her elbow, his bowtie already loosened. "It's basically obscene how good you are at this."

Sutton smoothed an invisible wrinkle in her black dress, the corners of her mouth lifting.

"Tell Valentina that."

As if summoned, Valentina appeared, all sharp cheekbones and sleek hair. Her gaze swept the room like a scanner, cataloging and approving.

"The staircase entrance worked," she said, satisfaction softening her strict tone. "And the lighting on the Cartier cases is perfect. Good work, Sutton."

Valentina's compliments were rare and folks often held them like collectibles.

Graham found her near the balcony, the city sprawling out beyond the glass in roaring silence. He handed her a flute of champagne; the bubbles caught the light from the chandelier overhead.

"You should be very proud" he said, nodding toward the room.

"Valentina seems happy," Sutton replied, watching guests glide through the space, each detail of the night moving like choreography she'd orchestrated. "That's what matters."

"And you?" Graham asked, profile lit by the city beyond. "Are you happy?"

The question caught her off guard. She turned to him, taking in the familiar lines of his face, the ease in his smile. There was no drama with Graham. No sharp edges of chaos. Their relationship fit neatly into shared calendars, weekend brunches, and "how was your day?" calls that never veered into uncomfortable territory.

Graham was steady like that. Practical, supportive, the kind of man who pre-booked reservations and sent follow-up emails no one had asked him to send. Life with him came in clean lines and clear expectations.

No one ever pointed a camera at them when they walked down the street. No one zoomed in on their hands to debate whether they were holding on too tightly.

It was peaceful.

"I am," she said. And she wasn't lying. Not entirely. "This is the work I've always wanted."

He watched her for a moment, something perceptive flickering behind his gaze, then lifted his glass.

"To the woman who makes impossible rooms work," he said.

She clinked her glass against his.

"To the man who somehow finds time to show up for all of it," she replied.

They smiled at each other.

But later, alone in her apartment, heels kicked off and her dress pooled at her feet, the quiet felt louder than it should have.

She padded barefoot to the kitchen, flicking on the under-cabinet lights. Her phone lay on the counter, screen dark.

On a whim, she opened a music app and set a playlist to shuffle while she searched the fridge for a drink.

The opening chords hit before she registered them.

In the end, it's not the fame,

Not a crowd that knows my name.

Her hand stilled on the cabinet handle.

She swallowed, lowering herself onto a barstool as Wesley's voice poured into the room, richer now, older somehow. The bridge wrapped around her like a familiar scent she'd thought she'd forgotten.

It's the touch of your hand,

The way you understand.

I'd give it all for us to stand.

She closed her eyes.

This song didn't feel like a direct line to her anymore. Too many people had claimed it since. But certain phrases still landed in the exact places she didn't want them to.

She played it again. And again. Seven times before she finally pressed pause.

Her phone lit with a new text from Brynn: *Have you seen this?* Followed by a link.

Curiosity won. She clicked.

The video opened on a late-night set. Wesley sat in a soft chair, hair a little longer, jaw dusted with stubble, fatigue tucked into the corners of his smile. The host leaned forward.

"So this new single, *Sacrifice*," he said. "People are calling it your most vulnerable song yet. Who or what is it about?"

Wesley's gaze flicked off-camera briefly, then returned.

"It's about a love that taught me more about myself than I ever knew," he said. "It's a part of me. Always will be."

Sutton snapped the laptop closed; the click was too loud in the quiet kitchen.

She stayed there for a long time, staring at the stainless-steel fridge, the magnet with her grocery list, the neat, curated life she'd built.

She had everything she'd told herself she wanted. Stability. Work she excelled at. A man who, the second time around, was finally showing up.

And yet, somewhere deep inside, a small, stubborn part of her still moved to the rhythm of a voice that no longer belonged to her.

***

They moved through separate lives, each chasing a different version of peace. Still, the imprint of what they'd shared remained, subtle, persistent, impossible to fully unlearn.

Thirty-Six

SUTTON TUGGED AT HER navy dress, the silk whispering against her skin as she and Graham stepped into the bar. Bass thumped under the low chatter, the kind that greased conversations and made strangers lean closer. The room smelled of oak, citrus peel, and something sweet from the kitchen fryer.

"Hey, there they are!"

Mike stood taller than she expected, in a navy suit, with that deliberately messy hair she recognized from Graham's photos.

When they reached the table, Graham introduced Sutton.

Handshakes, quick hugs, the scrape of chairs. Sutton sat beside Graham, his knee brushing hers beneath the table. Glass rings marked the wood. Fries arrived in a tin pail. Someone slid a fresh napkin beneath her drink like a quiet welcome.

Heads tipped toward her with curiosity but not scrutiny. Graham attached names from his stories to the faces around the table: Mike, his fiancée Janelle; Travis from the trivia team;

Rob with the band tattoos; Maya and Chris tucked shoulder to shoulder.

"Finally," Janelle said, smiling. "We have been hearing about you for weeks."

Sutton laughed.

"Only the edited highlights, I hope."

"Just enough to make the rest of us raise our standards," Mike said.

The table eased around her, conversation skipping across football scores and the mayor's press conference before landing on a citywide debate about the best dive bar. Graham slid a plate toward her without looking, as if it were muscle memory. She stole a fry. He pretended not to see, then stole one back.

Sutton felt herself let go of that nervous coil in her stomach. She watched Graham in his element, shoulders loose, hands sketching stories in the air, eyes crinkling at the corners when someone else landed a joke. He was magnetic without having to work at it. The room gave him space, and he used it to bring other people forward.

The server arrived with another round. Graham switched to soda water. Sutton noticed and smiled.

"Big meeting in the morning?" she teased.

"Big run," he said. "Mike is trying to prove he can still do eight miles without complaining."

"I never said without complaining," Mike said.

Janelle rolled her eyes, then turned her attention to Sutton. "So you're the art gallery mastermind."

"Mastermind is way overblown," Sutton said.

"She's underselling it," Graham said. "Her first curation was a hit."

Janelle nodded, satisfied. "Good. He needs someone who cares about things that are not investor calls."

"Hey," Graham said, hand over his heart. "Investors are everything."

Maya laughed.

"Now there's your next presentation title."

Sutton felt something in her chest loosen another notch. These were the people who saw Graham every day at work, and they included her without fuss. No weighing. No measuring. Just space made at the edge of the circle.

Sutton rested her chin on her hand and watched Graham listening to Mike. He listened the way he did everything, with his full attention. When he laughed, it drew a smile from her even though she'd missed the joke. It was easy. Quiet. It felt like something she could pick up again the next morning without first checking who she was.

On the walk out, Graham held the door and let the night lay itself around them. The sidewalk glowed wet from a quick rain. A taxi hissed by and threw light across the puddles. He took her hand as if he meant to keep it.

"Thoughts," he said. "Too much chaos for a school night?"

"I liked it," she said. "I liked them."

He squeezed once.

"They liked you."

She laughed.

"How can you tell?"

"You didn't flinch when Chris quoted a spreadsheet," he said. "That is the initiation."

They paused at the corner, the city air cool against her cheeks. Graham searched her face the way he did when he wanted to make sure the answer behind the answer matched the words.

"You okay?" he asked.

"I am," she said. "Tonight felt good."

"Good," he said, and leaned in to kiss her, not rushed, not a performance. Just the kind of kiss you can carry home without spilling.

They walked to the subway with fingers laced.

A dangerous question surfaced: *What would life have been like if they had never let go of each other a year ago?*

Thirty-Seven

Camera flashes burst like miniature suns as Wesley stepped out of the car, light fracturing across Arya's silver dress as she joined him. Her hand slid into the crook of his arm, poised and steady in the chaos.

"Arya, over here!"

Voices fired from every direction. Cameras clicked like teeth.

She turned, smiling with the ease of someone who had survived this attention, not chased it. Wesley let his public self settle across his shoulders.

"You look incredible tonight," he said, low, for her alone.

"Not so bad yourself."

Inside, the party buzzed with money, ambition, and champagne. Wesley guided her through the crowd, his fingers hovering a breath from her back.

"Is every one of these events like this?" Arya asked, scanning the room.

"Pretty much," he said. "Though the Dior party where we met might still be the most chaotic."

She laughed softly. "That photographer nearly knocked over the catering server."

"And you still managed to look like you planned it."

"Years of acting," she said with a shrug. "Looking calm while everything falls apart."

"Do you come to record label parties often?" she asked.

"More often than I'd like." His jaw eased the smallest bit. "This part is the job."

"It must be exhausting. Performing even when you're not onstage."

"It is." His voice softened. "Nights like this are easier with good company."

They moved from cluster to cluster. He shook hands. He answered questions. He laughed at the right places. His gaze kept straying back to Arya, who seemed to exist just to the side of the game. She listened more than she spoke. When a producer's laugh came with too many teeth, she stepped half a pace closer to Wesley, and he shifted to close the space, a small, easy shield that needed no words.

At the bar, she ordered a gimlet and thanked the bartender by name after reading his tag.

Later, at a quiet cocktail table just outside the main swirl, she asked, "Have you always known this would be your life?"

"Pretty much." He leaned on the table's edge. "Music gave me a voice when I didn't feel heard."

"I understand that." Her voice lowered. "Acting lets me live inside lives bigger than mine."

She watched him. Not the way people in this room watched a name. She watched as if she were waiting to see if his answer would match the shape.

"Do you think you'll ever tire of it?"

Truth crossed his face, quick and unguarded.

"Sometimes I think I already am."

"Then why keep going?"

He let out a quiet laugh through his nose. He looked past her to the room full of people trying too hard.

"What else would I do?"

"What the world expects of you doesn't define you. You could start over. It wouldn't even have to be music. You have that kind of presence."

Presence. The word staying longer in his mind even after the conversation moved on.

He smiled with no response.

"I am glad we made it to a fourth date," she whispered.

Wesley smiled, the expression practiced enough that no one watching would question it.

"Me too."

Thirty-Eight

Brynn's arms opened at the LAX arrival doors, her smile so wide it turned her eyes into half-moons. She crashed into Sutton with the force of a wave, vanilla perfume following as she squeezed her tight.

"Ah, I've missed you!"

Sutton laughed into her shoulder. The hug squeezed the travel fatigue out of her bones.

When they pulled apart, Brynn's gaze flicked over her, quick and assessing.

"You look chic, as always," she said, tucking a strand of hair behind Sutton's ear.

"So do you," Sutton said, her voice sincere.

In Brynn's convertible, the Los Angeles air whipped around them, carrying roadside flowers and the faint metallic tang of traffic. The city stretched wide as the sun dropped low, the light soft and hazy across the streets. Miles unwound like thread. Jokes overlapped. One half-finished story sparked another, and together they stitched themselves back into what they had always been.

At a red light on Sunset, Brynn let the gearshift go and covered Sutton's hand.

"So," she said, voice dropping under the music, "tell me what is going on with you."

The question floated between them, soft but immovable. Sutton traced a fray along her jacket hem and watched palm trees stencil the sky.

"There's nothing I can't handle," she said at last. "And definitely nothing that should bring down the weekend."

"Trust me," Brynn said. "By the time we are done with this weekend, whatever is bothering you will feel like it happened in another lifetime."

Sutton smiled. She didn't say that the real problem was geography. Somewhere in this sprawl, Wesley existed. She wouldn't run into him. She couldn't, possibly. Still, something restless stirred beneath her skin, a compass needle that refused to settle even as she tried to point it elsewhere.

Brynn's ivy-draped brick house rose ahead. Inside, it was all her: stacks of books against shelves of vinyl, throw pillows in impossible patterns, plants thriving despite benign neglect.

"Behold," Brynn announced, swinging open the fridge and producing a bottle like a game-show prize. "That Pinot you always finish too quickly. Truffle chips, you claim to hate, while inhaling the bag. And zero judgment of whatever we do or don't do."

They carried their wineglasses to the balcony.

"This," Brynn said, tapping her glass to Sutton's, "is exactly what the doctor ordered."

"Well, this and forty-eight hours of bachelorette duties for Gianna," Sutton said, swirling her wine. "We are here for the bride. Not just two degenerates on vacation."

"I cannot believe she is getting married," she added, shaking her head as a breeze caught her perfume. "I always thought we would beat her to the altar."

Brynn arched an eyebrow.

"Speak for yourself." She took a sip, voice warming. "He's good for her. Even if Paul is a carbon copy of her ex."

"Didn't she meet him at her ex's country club?" Sutton asked, dragging her chair closer.

"Full circle, honey," Brynn said, raising her glass again.

Brynn's thumb scrolled to an old playlist. Familiar beats drifted into the orange hour. As the sun slid into pinks and golds, Sutton felt her shoulders drop. For the first time in months, her mind was not calculating time zones, inboxes, or the statistical nightmare of running into a man in a city of millions. For now, the world belonged to a different life entirely.

***

Glen Ivy's steam rose like a promise and wrapped around them. Eucalyptus and sage lifted from the water. Sutton sank into the way down to her shoulders and felt heat move through her muscles, untying knots she had thought were permanent.

Around her, Gianna's bachelorette crew made a bright, noisy orbit. Laughter bounced off the water. Champagne flutes sparkled in the sun.

"To Gianna," Brynn called, raising her glass as condensation ran down her wrist. "May your marriage be as charming as the story of how you two found each other."

They cheered and clinked glasses. Gianna curtsied, theatrical and pink-cheeked, sending a ripple through the pool.

"Who knew my ex's country club membership would finally pay off?" she said, and they all laughed.

Sutton let her head fall against the warm stone edge and closed her eyes. Voices thinned to a soothing wash. The water did its quiet work, and for a while even her thoughts vanished.

The afternoon melted into hot pools and cool drinks, mud masks and languid stretches in the sun. Sutton's skin tingled. Her limbs felt heavy in a good way.

"BeachLife Festival is this weekend," Gianna announced suddenly, surging upright on her lounger. "We should go."

"Nah," Brynn said, deliberate and light. "Let's do Sunset Boulevard and dance."

Gianna shook her head, curls bouncing.

"Sunset is fun, but we can drink, dance, and flirt at BeachLife too."

Brynn's eyes found Sutton's across the deck. Something unspoken passed between them. Sutton frowned, not catching the signal.

"It could be fun," Sutton said, rolling her shoulders under the sun.

Emmy's thumbs flew over her phone. Sunglasses threw back squares of light.

"They have an impressive lineup tomorrow," she said, then stopped. "Wait."

She looked straight at Sutton.

"Didn't you date him?"

The air shifted. Sutton's stomach knotted. She glanced at Brynn. Brynn's mouth had gone tight.

"Yes," Gianna said, clapping once so her bangles chimed. "Wesley. That's right. You dated Wesley Preskott."

The name cracked across the deck. Sutton's mouth went dry.

Questions ricocheted before the first could land.

"Tell us everything," Mia said, eyes wide.

"Is he a good kisser?" Rachel asked, pushing her sunglasses down while sipping her drink.

"So which songs are about you?" Tasha leaned in, gleaming bright.

Brynn's lounge chair scraped against the pavers. Her voice was cool and even, like the morning tide.

"Leave her alone. It's not our business."

The deck went quiet in a way that was not actually quiet. Curiosity sat on the surface of every glance.

Gianna exhaled.

“Okay, okay. No questions.”

Silence held for a beat, broken only by the steady whir of the pool filter.

Then she smiled.

“But tomorrow...”

Brynn lifted her cocktail and didn’t look at anyone.

“Sunset would be fun,” she said. “I can get a reservation at Somni. You’ve wanted to try it.”

“No,” Gianna whined, tipping her head back. She leaned forward again, and the scent of coconut sunscreen rode with her, bright and sudden.

“BeachLife would be so much fun. Please, Sutton. It’s not like you’ll see him. Or that he’ll even know you’re there.”

All eyes turned. Sweat beaded along Sutton’s hairline despite the shade.

Gianna added. “He’ll be onstage. We’ll be in the crowd.”

Sutton looked at Brynn. Brynn gave the smallest shrug. It wasn’t defeat so much as recognition. The bride wanted a story.

“The bride wants what the bride wants,” Sutton said.

Cheers broke across the deck.

Plans blossomed at once, quick and messy. Wristbands. Rides. Outfits. Which shoes would survive in sand? Sutton eased back onto a lounger and slid on her sunglasses, grateful for the dark shield.

Behind the lenses, her breathing shortened. Every worst-case scenario lined up, patient as check-in. The mineral air filled her chest but couldn't reach the knot beneath her ribs.

Still, when Brynn passed her a fresh glass and bumped shoulders, Sutton managed a genuine smile.

"Cheers to focusing on tonight," Brynn said.

"To tonight," Sutton echoed.

The detonation could wait until tomorrow.

Thirty-Nine

The summer sun blazed over the festival, with waves breaking rhythmically against the shore. Bass thudded through Sutton's chest, a pulse that belonged more to the earth than the speakers. The air smelled of salt, sunscreen, and smoke from the food stalls curling into the sky.

She'd invented reasons not to come, but each excuse collapsed under the weight of Gianna's bachelorette joy. No matter how she framed it, skipping Gianna's celebration would brand her the friend who couldn't put someone else first, even for a weekend.

Neon posters plastered the entrance, the lineup stacked in bold fonts. But one name towered above the rest, printed in crimson letters so loud she could almost hear it:

Wesley Preskott.

By afternoon, they'd made it to the VIP section, a tangle of shade tents and low leather chairs. The view stretched wide, with crowds pulsing below, the ocean flashing between banners.

"At least enjoy the other bands," Brynn yelled over the music.

Sutton tried. She let Brynn drag her closer to the stage. The bass rose like a living thing beneath their feet. Brynn grabbed her hand, spinning her into the rhythm until they were both laughing, dizzy. Heat licked her skin; whiskey loosened her edges. For a moment, the world was all light and sound, until it wasn't.

"Taking the main stage now, Wesley Preskott!"

The words landed like a physical blow. Sutton froze mid-turn. Around her, the crowd erupted, but her body wouldn't move.

Gianna and friends darted toward the stage, their excited squeals trailing behind them like ribbons.

Brynn's grip tightened, steady but wordless.

"We can leave..."

"I'm fine," Sutton said, though her throat was dry. "Go on. He's your friend too."

Brynn hesitated, reading the truth in her eyes.

"If you change your mind.""

"I won't," Sutton said softly.

She wanted this moment to herself. She wanted to feel it, to face it, alone.

Brynn disappeared into the surge of bodies. Sutton stood at the edge, where the sound hit, but the lights couldn't reach her. The first chord cut through the air, familiar and foreign at once. His voice followed, raw and grounded, carrying all the weight she'd tried to bury.

Each lyric peeled something open. Every memory she'd folded small came unstuck.

When the music softened, Wesley leaned toward the mic.

"Thanks for coming out tonight. I've missed this." He ran a hand through his hair, a familiar gesture she used to tease him about. "This next one's called Sacrifice, the first single off the record, and it's about that moment when your whole life gets turned upside down by something you never saw coming; something that makes you question everything you thought you knew about what matters."

The first note struck, and the world shifted. Sutton felt it in her ribs, the ache of recognition, the sting of memory disguised as melody. His voice cracked somewhere in the bridge, and the imperfection undid her. He'd once told her real music lived in the flaws. She understood that now.

When the final chord faded, the crowd erupted. Wesley ran across the stage, reaching out as hands shot up toward him, laughing as he tried to high-five them all. Near the left side, where the VIP crowd pressed close to the barricade, he paused, his smile widening into something bright and boyish. He waved toward someone in the crowd, and the response was deafening. Sutton didn't need to guess; Brynn's golden hair and Gianna's excited screams were impossible to miss.

She turned away, irrationally certain he could see her from a mile off. He couldn't, even so, something in her wanted to hide.

Around her, the crowd scattered for drinks and bathroom breaks, its pulse dimming into the night. Sutton walked with no destination, the air growing heavier the farther she moved from the stage, as though gravity had finally remembered her again.

Back in the VIP tent, Brynn was waiting with two drinks and an expression that said everything.

"Want to leave?" she asked quietly.

Sutton shook her head.

"I'm okay."

She wasn't. Not yet. But she didn't want to leave either.

They sank into one of the low chairs. Ice melted in their glasses as the festival blurred around them. Then Brynn's phone buzzed. She glanced at it, then looked up.

"Wesley's asking where I am," she said. "He doesn't know you're here. Do you want me to make an excuse?"

Sutton's mouth was dry.

"No," she said after a pause.

Gianna squealed from across the table, already tipsy on beer and sun.

"Oh my God, Sutton, you have to say hi! It's my last weekend of freedom; don't ruin my chance to meet a literal rock star."

Brynn frowned, fingers hovering.

"You sure?"

Sutton forced a smile.

"Yeah. Why not?"

***

Wesley arrived at the VIP tent, where Brynn said she'd be. The space buzzed with the easy chaos that always followed a show. Laughter spilled over the bass from the main stage, cocktail glasses clinked, and someone shouted across the crowd for another round.

He hadn't planned to stay long, just a quick hello, maybe a drink, then back to his house. The adrenaline from the performance still thrummed under his skin, soft and restless.

Heads turned when he stepped inside. It was familiar, the quick ripple of attention, the flash of phones. He smiled out of reflex, nodding as people called his name, the sound of it blurred by the music.

Then he spotted Brynn near the back, waving him over with that bright, unbothered grin that always made things feel easier. He started toward her, already forming something light to say.

And then he saw her.

The breath left his chest so fast it almost startled him.

Sutton.

She was standing just beside Brynn, a glass in her hand, the light catching in her hair like it always used to. For a beat, he thought he was imagining her, a trick of exhaustion or memory, but then she looked up.

"Wesley, hey!"

Brynn's voice snapped him back. She was on her feet, grinning, motioning him over.

He crossed the tent automatically, but every step pulled him closer to the one thing he hadn't been ready for.

Brynn gestured down the line of faces, naming them as if she hadn't just detonated something between them.

"And of course," she said, softer now, "you already know Sutton."

He turned fully.

Her eyes met his, cautious but curious, steady enough to undo him. He caught the minor tremor in her fingers around the glass, the way she swallowed before speaking.

"Hey," she said, barely more than a breath.

"Hey."

Gianna filled the space instantly, gushing about his set, her excitement tumbling over itself. He smiled, nodded, performed again, but every nerve in his body was taut with tension toward Sutton.

She didn't look up again, and somehow that hurt worse.

When Gianna and the others finally drifted toward the bar, the surrounding noise thinned to a steady hum. Sutton stayed behind, pretending to watch the next band tune up.

She felt him before she heard him.

"You look..."

Wesley's voice came from just behind her, rough from the set, threaded with hesitation. He stopped a few feet away, shaking his head with a faint, incredulous smile. "It's strange. Seeing you here."

She laughed quietly, the sound small against everything going on around them.

"I didn't know you were here," he said. "Or in L.A."

"I saw your name on the lineup," she admitted, eyes on her glass. "I almost didn't come."

He hesitated, the faintest smile pulling at his mouth.

"But you did."

"I did."

For a moment, neither of them spoke, the crowd surging and fading around them. He shifted slightly, hands in his pockets.

"How are you?" he asked at last, his tone light and careful, small talk meant to sound easy.

"I'm good," she said, though it came out thinner than she meant. "You?"

"Busy," he admitted, with a quiet laugh undercutting the word. "That always seems to be my answer."

The crowd blurred into color and sound, everything else fading to static.

From somewhere near the bar, Gianna's voice cut through the noise, bright and final.

"Sutton! Time to go!"

Sutton turned toward the sound, then back to him.

"I should..."

"Yeah." His voice was low. "It's good to see you."

"You too."

He didn't mean to step forward, but he did. The hug was brief, careful, the kind that remembers more than it allows. Her perfume brushed his collar, and for half a second, he forgot how to exhale.

When she pulled away, his fingers twitched as if they struggled between wanting to hold on and knowing better.

"How long are you here?" he asked.

"A few more days."

He nodded slowly, not knowing what to do with that.

She took a few steps back, a soft, genuine, fleeting smile touching her lips. For a moment, she looked both happy to see him and quietly sorry to leave.

Her hand lifted in a small wave. She mouthed *bye,* the word catching on a breath he couldn't hear. Two more steps, then she turned, swallowed by the crowd.

Wesley stood where she'd left him, the noise swelling back like a tide. Someone called his name; another hand clapped his shoulder. He smiled automatically, but the gesture felt off, slightly delayed, as if part of him was still watching the space she'd just disappeared into.

Forty

California sunlight dappled across Wesley's kitchen table, warming the ceramic mug between his palms. Steam curled from the coffee, but he barely noticed as he stared at the unsent message on his phone.

Coffee before you leave LA?

His thumb hovered. Yesterday's encounter with Sutton replayed in fragments: windswept dark hair, sunlight catching in her eyes when she'd finally looked at him. He hesitated a beat longer, then pressed send. The soft whoosh filled the quiet. The message was gone, already crossing the city. Wesley turned his phone face down, the click of it on wood punctuating what couldn't be undone.

Across town, Sutton's phone vibrated against the marble counter. Wesley's name lit the screen, sending a jolt through her chest. She read the message twice, her bagel cooling on its plate.

She stared at the text, pretending to weigh her answer while her heart had already decided. Her thumbs hovered, deleting and retyping three times before settling on:

I'd like that. I have some free time this afternoon if you are.

His reply arrived before she could set the phone down.

Perfect. My place is close to the biking trail I mentioned once, the one with the city view. We could meet at my house, then walk there together?

Sutton typed back.

Sounds good. Text me your address. See you this afternoon.

She placed the phone down deliberately.

"Well, well." Brynn's voice came from the hallway. Hair twisted in a towel, she leaned against the doorframe, grinning.

"What's that smile about?"

"Just meeting Wesley for coffee later," Sutton said, rearranging the fruit bowl.

Brynn arched a brow.

"So who made the first move this time, you or him?"

"He texted me."

Sutton tried to sound casual, but the corner of her mouth curved up.

Brynn bit into an apple, eyes glinting.

"Look at you two. Right back where you started, aren't you?"

***

An hour later, Sutton stood outside Wesley's house, iced coffee in hand. The nerves she'd ignored on the drive over finally caught up with her. She exhaled once, then knocked.

The door opened almost immediately. Wesley stood barefoot in jeans and a fitted tee, with the ease that came naturally to him.

"Your iced coffee," she said, handing it over.

His familiar smile greeted her.

"Afternoon caffeine's non-negotiable."

Sutton stepped inside. The house offered a grounded, open atmosphere. He'd made peace here; she could feel it.

"I like it," she said. "It feels very you."

"Funny," he said, glancing over with a half-smile. "That's exactly what I said about your place in New York."

She smirked, the spark of their old banter flickering to life.

"Fair."

He jingled his keys; the sound filled the pause between them.

"Ready to go? I've been cooped up all day," he said, unlocking the door. Then, after a small beat, "I can give you a tour when we get back."

They strolled along a tree-lined street where light filtered through leaves in restless patterns. Their steps synced naturally, as though the time between them had never stretched so far.

"So," he said after a while, glancing at her, "how've you been?"

Sutton hesitated. There were too many possible answers.

"Things are moving along," she said finally. "Work's steady. The art showcase I curated a few months back was a highlight."

"Right, the showcase. I'm sorry I missed it. How'd it go?"

Her eyes brightened as she talked about the turnout, the energy, and the sold pieces.

"Better than I imagined."

"I'm not surprised." His voice gentled. "You're talented. I'm glad people are seeing it."

Something in his sincerity landed deeper than she expected.

"Thanks," she murmured.

To change the subject, she asked, "And you? The album, the tour?"

"Busy," he admitted. "Everything's moving fast."

"Well, *Sacrifice* is incredible," she said. "Raw. Honest. Hard to listen to, but beautiful."

"Only hard because you know too much," he teased.

"Maybe," she said, smiling faintly.

They turned a corner onto a hill where the city stretched beneath them, glowing gold in the late afternoon.

"This is where I come to breathe," he said quietly. "To think."

She didn't answer, though she felt the sting of understanding. His life was steady now. Rebuilt. Slightly out of reach.

They sat on a bench. For a while, neither spoke.

"I'm glad we did this," she said at last. "Just being here. With you."

"Yeah," he said. "I've missed this. Talking to you."

Sutton smiled faintly, the breeze catching her hair.

"We used to talk about everything. Even the things that didn't matter."

"Those were my favorite," he said, his mouth tilting. "The ones that didn't matter. They always ended up mattering anyway."

She nudged his arm lightly.

"You mean arguing about playlists and whether breakfast counts as dinner?"

He laughed under his breath.

"Exactly that. You always won."

"I was usually right."

"Usually," he said, glancing over at her. "But sometimes I just enjoyed hearing you talk."

The air stilled, not awkward, just full. The kind of quiet that didn't need filling. She looked toward the view, sunlight bleeding through the haze.

"Feels different now," she said. "Calmer."

"Maybe we needed different first," he said softly.

She turned to him, the honesty in his tone settling deep.

"Maybe we did."

Their walk back was lighter. They laughed easily, their rhythm rediscovered but fragile.

By the time they reached his door, the sun had dropped low, spilling long streaks of evening light across the pavement. Wesley paused, keys in hand.

"Want to come in for that tour?"

Sutton smiled, the kind that held both temptation and restraint.

"I should go. But thank you. For today."

He nodded once, then stepped forward and pulled her in. The hug wasn't long, but it was genuine, uncomplicated. For a moment, it felt like the past and present had learned how to breathe the same air.

When they parted, he said quietly, "Don't be a stranger."

"You too," she said, her voice soft but certain.

This wasn't about what they'd been, or even what they might still be. It was about remembering they could share the same space without unraveling.

FORTY-ONE

BACK IN NEW YORK, Sutton's fingers drummed against her thigh as she checked the time again, seven minutes since she last looked. Graham would arrive any moment. She paced to the window, then back to the mirror where she tucked a strand of hair behind her ear, then untucked it. She had missed him, his steadiness, his gentle way of looking at her.

When the knock finally came, her heart skipped as she crossed the apartment in three quick strides, fingers fumbling with the lock.

Her smile bloomed as she opened the door.

"Hey, you."

Graham didn't waste a second, stepping inside and capturing her lips in an immediate, consuming kiss. His hands found her waist, fingers spreading wide as he pulled her close, like he'd been starving for this moment all day.

"I missed you," he murmured, his voice low, a reassuring anchor amid the otherwise buzzing energy of the moment.

She pulled back just enough to meet his gaze, her lips still tingling from his kiss.

"It's only been five days."

"Five days were too long." His thumb traced lazy circles on her hip. "I kept thinking about this mouth of yours during my conference call."

A laugh bubbled up from her chest.

"That's terrible for productivity."

"Worth every distracted minute." He pressed another kiss to the corner of her mouth, then her jaw. "Besides, Johnson was droning on about quarterly projections. You're infinitely more interesting."

Her fingers curled deeper into his shirt, anchoring herself as his lips worked magic along her neck.

"Smooth talker," she whispered, but her body betrayed how much his words affected her, arching into his touch.

His eyes found hers as he lifted his head.

"I save all my best lines for you," he murmured, the corner of his mouth lifting in a way that made her stomach flutter.

Eventually, they untangled themselves, and Graham reached for his overnight bag and set it by the staircase. He turned back to her with a soft, sated smile.

"So tell me about California," he said, running a hand through his disheveled hair. "How's Brynn doing?"

"It was nice," Sutton answered, careful in her response. "It's always good to see Brynn and catch up." She paused, then added lightly, "It was a whirlwind, though."

A flicker of guilt tugged at her for omitting the whole truth. Mentioning Wesley wouldn't help anything.

He nodded, accepting her explanation at face value.

"And Brynn?"

"She's good," Sutton said, leading him toward the kitchen. "Oh, and Alexander might finally move in with her."

"No way." Graham halted mid-step, eyebrows rising. "For those two? It's about time," he said with a laugh, shaking his head. "They've been circling each other forever."

Sutton chuckled, opening the fridge.

"Right? It's a miracle they've lasted this long without killing each other. But somehow, it works."

He leaned casually against the counter, his calm, perceptive eyes always making her feel seen.

"And you? How are you?"

There was a gentleness in his tone, direct yet caring.

Sutton paused, meeting his gaze.

"I'm better now," she said, acknowledging the moment between them again. "It was nice to get away for a bit. To reset."

"Reset," he echoed, a small smile on his lips.

"Just a bit," she admitted, returning his smile and handing him a bottle of sparkling water.

He cracked it open, taking a sip before speaking.

"What do you say, Indian for dinner? I've been craving curry again."

"Curry it is," Sutton replied, her voice brightening.

But Graham stepped closer, brushing her cheek instead of drifting toward the takeout menus. His thumb traced the curve of her jaw, and his gaze softened as he looked at her.

"I'm glad you're back," he murmured, voice low and almost reverent.

Sutton barely had time to respond before he kissed her, slow and deep. She sank into it, her fingers tangling in his hair as he guided her to the couch with a gentle urgency simmering beneath. Their kisses deepened, motions turning instinctive as they rediscovered the intimacy they'd once shared.

Graham's hands traveled over her back, steadying her as she straddled his lap, body melting into his. When he pulled back, resting his forehead against hers, his breath was warm against her skin in the quiet space between them.

"Never leave New York again," he murmured, raw emotion edging his voice. "It's torture."

Sutton's heart twisted at his vulnerability. She didn't respond with words. Instead, she kissed him again, palms sliding up his chest, drawing closer. The way he steadied her hips, the way he held her as though he needed her to breathe, made her ache in unexpected ways.

Graham's fingers grazed the hem of her blouse, hesitating as though asking for permission. Sutton raised her arms, allowing him to lift it away with deliberate care. Cool air brushed her exposed skin, replaced quickly by the warmth of his hands on her waist.

She pulled his shirt over his shoulders, their movements growing more urgent.

“Look what you do to me,” Graham murmured against her neck, voice low and thick with desire. “I need all of you.”

He trailed kisses along her skin, slow and deliberate. Sutton arched into him, her fingers in his hair, guiding him closer.

They moved in a rhythm of trust and familiarity, rediscovering one another in a way only those who had previously dated could. Clothes fell aside, scattered like forgotten barriers, until nothing but touch stood between them. Their breaths merged, every movement deepening the connection.

Later, they lay entwined on the couch, Sutton’s bare legs tangled with his beneath the throw blanket she’d hastily pulled over them. Outside, the sun had already surrendered to early darkness, leaving only the warm glow of her reading lamp to cast long shadows across the hardwood floor.

Graham’s arm rested across her waist, his fingertips sketching figure eights on the sensitive skin just above her hip, sending pleasant shivers up her spine.

“I’ve worked up quite an appetite. I think it’s time we order.”

Sutton’s laugh echoed against the walls as she disentangled herself, fishing her blouse from where it had landed on the coffee table. She pulled it over her head, her hair falling in messy waves.

“I’ll order,” she said, tapping her phone screen, “but we’re not getting six orders of garlic naan like last time.”

He pushed himself up on one elbow; the blanket sliding down to reveal his chest.

"The delivery guy thought I was having a party."

"You were having a carb party," she quipped, settling back beside him, her shoulder pressed against his as she scrolled through familiar menu items.

The weight against her side felt like a puzzle piece clicking into place, the small domestic moment more intimate than what had come before.

Forty-Two

The sun woke the edges of Arya's room and slid across Wesley's bare shoulders. He pressed a kiss to her temple carefully, then eased out of bed. The house held an early hush that felt almost like permission.

In the kitchen, he poured a coffee and leaned against the counter, setting his phone facedown as tour dates chased each other across his thoughts.

The phone buzzed. He flipped it over without thinking.

Sutton's name lit the screen.

"How did I miss this when I was in LA?"

A photo followed. Some stranger's hand held up a cup with his name on it in supermarket font. *The Wesley Preskott smoothie.* Erewhon had turned him into something edible.

He laughed into his mug and typed.

"It's pretty good. Next time, you'll have to stop by and get one."

Her text bubble appeared immediately.

"You forget, I already know what you taste like, Mr. Preskott."

The coffee went down the wrong way. He coughed, smiling at the sudden punch of memory. Her timing. The way she could flick the light on in a room he had left dark.

"Oh, trust me, I didn't forget."

He stared at the last line for a second too long.

His thumbs were already moving.

"Hey, I forgot to tell you I'm in town this weekend for SNL. Are you around on Sunday?"

He set the phone down and took a long drink.

The phone buzzed.

"I can't meet up on Sunday. I have a five-year-old's birthday party to go to. Maybe... I can join you for the SNL taping?"

"Really? You'd be into that?"

"Sure. I mean, if you're up to it. It would be cool to support you. Plus, I've never seen a live taping."

The room tilted slightly. Not the old rush, but close enough to notice.

"That sounds good to me. I'll give Kevin a heads-up. Can't wait to see you."

He texted Kevin to put her on the list for tickets and backstage passes, then told himself to stop checking his phone.

Arya padded in wearing one of his shirts, eyes soft with sleep, and slid her arms around his waist from behind. He sucked in a breath, surprised at how the day could hold two truths at once and make room for both. She pressed her cheek against his shoulder blades.

"You're up early," she murmured.

"Time zone changes are killing me," he said, leaving it there.

She let go to hunt for cereal, humming something that might end up in a trailer in three months. He watched her move through the kitchen as if she owned every room she entered. He had always admired that in her. The cheerful lack of crisis.

He finished his coffee and set the mug in the sink.

This was simple. Just a friend at a show.

He told himself that twice.

Forty-Three

Saturday moved like a metronome set one click too fast. Rehearsal. Camera blocking. A note from the musical director. A text from Kevin reminding him to save his voice for the night. A surprise punch of nerves that had nothing to do with nerves and everything to do with a name on the guest list.

Within an hour, he had found the pocket. The song held. His hands did what they were supposed to do. The host nailed the political cold open. In the hallway outside his dressing room, he caught sight of himself in a framed photo from another season, younger by a lifetime, jaw tight, eyes bright with a hunger he had long since fed and replaced with something else.

Twenty minutes before live. The room was suddenly all fluorescent edges and too many mirrors. He rolled his shoulders and shook out his hands.

Knock.

Kevin stuck his head in.

"She's here." No preamble.

Wesley felt the hit in his ribs. He nodded as if it were nothing.

"Cool."

Kevin smirked.

"You good?"

"I'm always good."

"You're not always good."

Wesley laughed once and turned to his guitar.

"I'm good enough."

"Want me to walk her to friends and family?"

He pictured it: the turn in the hallway, the shift in the light, her coat folded in her lap, the way she'd sit a little straighter when the band started. He shook his head.

"Yeah. Thanks. Tell her I'll see her after."

"You sure?"

Wesley didn't look up.

"If I see her before, I'm not going to hear the first verse."

Kevin left. The room went quiet in that thick backstage way, a silence that knows what's coming.

Five minutes. He closed his eyes and let the first line find him, the one he could sing half-drunk, fully asleep, or on fire.

Two minutes. Guitar strap over his shoulder. The hallway smelled of dust and hairspray and history. The floor vibrated beneath him, alive like a heartbeat.

He walked out under the lights and didn't look for her.

In the audience, Sutton pressed her knees together and tried to breathe with the crowd. The band struck a few bright notes that shivered through the bleachers. A red light blinked awake on a camera.

"Ladies and gentlemen, tonight's musical guest, Wesley Preskott."

Light broke across the stage. He stepped into it with a guitar and brushed the mic stand with his thumb. The first chord spilled out clean. The second followed, and the room leaned with him. Sutton found herself leaning too.

The melody gathered itself and lifted. His voice found the register he saved for honest rooms, the one that sounded like midnight kitchens and half-finished confessions. Around her, strangers swayed. She heard only him.

"I thought I could leave it all behind,
the lights, the fame, the endless grind.
But in the quiet of the night,
your memory keeps its light."

Her hands tightened over each other in her lap. For a heartbeat, she did not know if she wanted to cry or stand and walk out. She did neither. She watched him give shape to something they had both already lived.

He let the song carry, eyes closed on the longest note, jaw flexing as if the truth cost something to lift. The band fell in behind him, restrained, respectful. The last chord hung, then settled. Silence held for a breath, then the room broke open with applause.

He exhaled as if the music had loosened a knot in his chest. He smiled once, small and real, and the lights dipped.

After the show, backstage was chaos again, the echo of adrenaline still hanging in the air. Someone yelled, " Wardrobe!" Wesley scanned the blur of faces until he found her near the edge of it all, standing beside Kevin.

Her expression said everything before she spoke.

"You were amazing as always," she said when he reached her, eyes bright.

He smiled, still catching his breath, the pulse of the performance lingering in him.

"Thanks," he said quietly. "I'm glad you were here."

Kevin clapped his shoulder, grinning. "Hell of a show, man." Then he turned to Sutton. "You heading to the after-party?"

She blinked, surprised, before Wesley stepped in.

"Oh, right. I forgot to tell you." He rubbed the back of his neck. "There's an after-party. I kind of have to make an appearance. Want to come?"

Sutton hesitated, her smile wavering. She hadn't realized they'd be parting ways so soon.

"Those things aren't really my scene," she admitted, glancing at the clock on the wall. A quiet laugh escaped her. "I'm usually asleep by now."

"No pressure. But it'd be nice to have you there. Even just for a bit."

She weighed it, then nodded.

"Okay. Just for a bit."

***

The lounge's low light turned glasses into small moons, glinting whenever someone laughed too loudly. Conversations braided with bass lines. Sutton stayed close to Wesley as he introduced her to the cast and bandmates, his hand resting briefly at the small of her back.

"How's Arya? We were supposed to go to Stagecoach," an actress asked him casually.

Sutton's fingers tightened around the wine stem before she even registered the motion. Her expression remained perfectly still.

"She's good," Wesley said easily. "Filming in Australia."

The actress nodded, then glanced just once at Sutton.

"And you two, how do you know each other?"

"We've been friends for a while," Sutton said. Smooth. Clean. Deceptively easy.

"Real friends are rare here," the actress replied, smiling as she drifted away.

The moment she was gone, Wesley's voice dropped. "You okay?"

"Sure, why wouldn't I be?" She forced a smile, showing no emotion.

"Come on," he murmured, guiding her toward the edge of the room, to the glass where the city spilled light like molten silver across the Hudson.

They found two low chairs. Distance.

"This view," she whispered, setting her glass on her knee.

"Hard to beat New York beauty," he answered, though he was looking at her, not the skyline.

"So... Arya?"

A faint smile tugged at his mouth. He glanced down, tracing the seam of his pants with his thumb.

Sutton's voice stayed gentle, curious rather than prying.

"She's beautiful."

"She is," he said after a moment. "We're still figuring things out." His gaze lifted, steady and unreadable. "We're alike in some ways."

Sutton turned back toward the skyline, though her smile stayed in place. The words landed sharper than she expected.

"Well," she said softly, "I'm glad. Things have to fit to work."

"And you?" he asked quietly. "Anyone you're figuring out?"

She hesitated, then met his eyes.

"Graham, actually

Wesley nodded slowly, the movement small, but he felt it. A quiet exhale.

"Look at you keeping secrets."

"My life doesn't end up in tabloids," she replied, a small smile returning.

He huffed a breath, not quite laughter.

"Touché." He lifted his glass. "To second chances."

Her glass met his with the softest click.

"To finding what works."

For a moment they just watched the city lights stitched across the window.

Wesley spoke first.

"I've wondered, was it just the fame that broke us?"

"No," she said gently. "Not just that."

"Then what?" His brow softened, not defensive, just asking.

She hesitated.

"I lost myself," she said quietly. "In us. In your world. I was afraid I'd stop being me and become your shadow. Everything I'd built felt like it might disappear. I didn't know how to hold both."

His expression flickered, regret, then something softer.

"I never wanted that. I wanted you to shine. I still do."

"I know." She looked down at her hand on the glass. "But back then, I couldn't see that. I needed space with no one else's name attached."

He sat with that. The silence between them didn't strain. It exhaled.

"Thank you for saying it," he murmured. "I'm glad we can have this kind of honesty now."

For a moment neither moved.

Around them, the after-party thinned.

They rose without speaking, not walking away from anything, simply no longer needing to stay.

Outside, the city moved at a lower hum.

"This feels like a good step," she said. "Being friends. Something we never really tried."

"Yeah," he said. "I like this too."

They stood together under the same light, telling the truth without asking anything more of it.

Perhaps it was possible to exist in separate lives.

Forty-Four

Sutton and Graham's drive to the Catskills was a welcome escape from the city's relentless pulse. The winding roads curved through moss-dark trees as the skyline shrank in the rearview mirror. Laughter filled the car, blending with the steady rhythm of the engine as if they were already halfway to another life.

"This place is perfect for the weekend."

Sutton stepped out of the car. The air was crisp enough to taste. It slipped into her lungs, clearing the last of the city from her chest.

Graham grinned, hands in his coat pockets.

"I knew you'd like it."

The cabin was modest, warm, and every surface was amber by lamplight.

By nightfall, dinner simmered on the stove, firelight flickered against the cedar walls, and a deep stillness settled around them like thick wool.

"This is exactly what we needed," Graham said, sinking into the couch beside her. "Just a weekend for us."

"It is," Sutton agreed, her body softening into the cushions. "It's nice."

They talked for hours about nothing urgent, nothing heavy. Sutton felt a rare sense of calm settle over her.

She could have told him then. About Wesley. About SNL. About the thing she had kept small on purpose.

She didn't.

Morning arrived with the smell of coffee before the light.

"Good morning, beautiful," he said, leaning down to kiss her forehead.

Sutton smiled, surprised but smitten.

"What's all this?"

"Breakfast in bed for my favorite person." He set the tray on her lap like it was nothing, like loving her was easy.

It almost was.

They ate slowly, laughing between bites. Normal. Safe. Sweet in the way most people pray love will be.

Sutton slipped away to the bathroom, combing her fingers through her hair. When she stepped back into the bedroom, Graham sat on the edge of the bed, her phone in his hand.

It was still buzzing.

Wesley's name glowed on the screen.

Her lungs stalled.

"It started ringing," he said quickly, holding the phone out to her. "I didn't mean to—"

"I know." Her voice was steady but thin.

He hesitated, searching her face.

"Are you and Wesley talking again?"

There was no accusation in his voice. That was somehow worse.

"Yes," Sutton said quietly. No scrambling. No lying. "But it's not what you think."

Graham stood, his jaw flexing.

"How long?"

"Since L.A.," she admitted. "At the bachelorette. Then I saw him last weekend. Just to talk."

Silence held between them like glass.

"You saw him last weekend," he repeated, "and I'm finding out now."

"I didn't think it mattered," she said too quickly. "I didn't want to make it into something it isn't. He's with someone else. Arya. We're just trying to be friends."

Graham let out a soft laugh, disbelief fraying the sound.

"You didn't think it mattered? Sutton... Wesley isn't just an ex."

"I didn't want to complicate this," she insisted, her voice trembling. "You're who I'm with. You're who I want."

"Then why hide him from me?" His voice didn't rise, but something inside it cut. "If it meant nothing, you wouldn't have."

Sutton felt her pulse pounding in her throat.

"I didn't want to hurt you."

"But you did," he said quietly.

She opened her mouth, but no words came.

Graham exhaled slowly and reached for his jacket.

"I need some air."

"Graham—"

"I'll be back."

The door shut gently behind him.

Forty-Five

Sutton eased into her workday the next morning, their early return from the Catskills still lingering in her thoughts. As she worked through her inbox and calendar, the rhythm of routine offered fragile peace until Mark's voice cut through it.

"Look what's floating around the internet," he teased, leaning over her desk with a mischievous grin.

On his phone: Sutton and Wesley, caught by a paparazzi lens, leaving the SNL studio's back door. The photo's angle and their proximity suggested more intimacy than friendship.

Sutton's eyes widened for a fraction of a second before she composed herself.

"We're just friends," she said firmly, brushing off his grin.

She hadn't even noticed cameras that night, a sharp contrast to when she'd dated Wesley and was hyperaware of every lens. The urgency to hide was gone, replaced by surprising indifference.

Mark arched his brows at her.

"That's all I get? No juicy scoop?"

"Nothing to tell," Sutton replied, offering a dismissive smile. "Now, if you don't mind..."

Mark wandered off, disappointed, leaving her alone with the image burned into her mind.

Curiosity itched at her until she gave in. She opened her browser and typed *Wesley Preskott news.*

Instantly, headlines exploded across her screen:

Wesley Preskott Spotted With Mystery Woman After SNL!

Is Wesley's New Album Inspired by a Rekindled Romance?

She leaned back and exhaled. It wasn't just the photos. There were speculations, unnamed sources, entire threads weaving fiction from fragments. Some articles even questioned Wesley's relationship with Arya, hinting at cracks that might not exist.

A wry smile tugged at her lips. She copied one of the more absurd links and sent it to Wesley.

"The news is sure creative, haha."

His reply came almost instantly.

"Yeah, there's a lot of those floating around. You okay? I know how much you hated this kind of attention."

It's all nonsense, and I'm fine. Feels different now. Just noise.

But when she set her phone down, unease flickered beneath the surface. She might not care about the headlines, but Graham could see them. And after the weekend in the Catskills, this might be the fracture that finally broke things.

Determined to be upfront with Graham, Sutton reopened her messages.

"Heads up, some silly tabloid stuff about Wesley and me from SNL is floating around. It's total nonsense, but I wanted you to hear it from me first. Can we talk later?"

She hesitated, then pressed send.

Honesty came with its own risks. Would Graham understand? Their balance already felt fragile.

Minutes crawled by. She buried herself in emails, each notification pulling her attention back to her silent phone. Every buzz made her pulse jump, only to fall again when it wasn't him.

Finally, she couldn't take it anymore. She dialed his number. Each ring stretched longer than the last.

"Hey, it's me," she said quietly. "Just checking in. Call when you can."

She ended the call and stared at the screen.

She'd tried to reach him.

But his silence said more than anger ever could.

***

Wesley sat at the head of the long conference table, fingers drumming a restless pattern against the polished wood as voices ricocheted around him. Logistics coordinators debated venues.

His lighting director argued with the tour accountant. Kevin scrolled through a tablet, rattling off routing options.

It was all familiar, the machinery of a life he'd once thrived inside. Yet today it felt like sitting too close to a speaker turned one notch past comfortable.

"Wes," Kevin said, glancing up. "Tokyo. Are we approving the second show?"

Wesley scanned the spreadsheet, lines of cities blurring together.

"Yeah," he said. "Go for it."

"And London?"

Kevin's tone was tentative.

Wesley exhaled through his nose.

"Two nights. Full production."

The conversation rushed forward, a torrent he rode effortlessly. Now it tugged at him like an undertow, subtle but persistent. By the time the meeting wrapped and assistants filed out, the room finally exhaled.

Kevin lingered behind, collecting stray notes.

"You good?" he asked, not as a manager, but as someone who'd known Wesley before all this. Before the arenas, before the burnout, before the hiatus that had nearly broken him.

Wesley leaned back in his chair, letting his eyes drift to the massive tour calendar on the wall. A roadmap of the months he'd be spending everywhere except home.

"Yeah," he said. "Just a lot happening fast."

Kevin slid into the seat across from him.

"That used to be your favorite part."

Wesley's mouth twitched.

"Used to be."

Kevin nodded slowly, letting silence fill the cracks.

"You've been back, what, six months? After almost a year off the grid? That's practically a rebirth in this business."

Wesley chuckled under his breath.

"You could say that."

"How's it feel?" Kevin asked quietly. "Being back in the noise again?"

Wesley paused. Really paused.

Most people asked about numbers. Ticket sales, streams, press.

Not how it felt.

Nobody asked about the noise.

"It's loud," he finally said. "Not just the music. Everything. The interviews. The pressure. The timelines. The expectation of being 'on' all the time. Even when it's good, it's loud."

Kevin huffed a dry laugh.

"How's Arya with all this? The schedule, the intensity?"

Wesley's jaw tightened, not out of anger but guilt.

"She's amazing," he said truthfully. "Supportive. Busy with her own projects. High energy as ever."

"But?" Kevin pressed, his tone gentle, not prying.

Wesley exhaled through his nose.

"She thrives in the chaos. Like I used to."

Kevin nodded, not surprised.

"She wants more time together?"

"Not really," Wesley admitted. "She's independent. But even then, we're always passing each other mid-flight. FaceTiming from hotel rooms. It's fine. Easy. But I don't know. I can't feel my life in it. Not like I used to."

Kevin's eyebrows lifted.

"You think it's her? Or everything else swallowing you whole?"

Wesley didn't answer right away.

When he finally spoke, his voice was low.

"It's me. It's the whole damn machine. Arya's great. Better than I deserve, probably."

"Well, you're writing again," Kevin observed. "Showing up. Doing the work. But you look overloaded. Like you're climbing a hill you're not sure you want to get to the top of."

Wesley swallowed. The inside of his ribcage felt tight.

"I'm grateful," he said. "For all of it. But sometimes I feel like I'm stepping right back into the life that burned me out in the first place. And I keep asking myself whether I'm actually ready."

"That's the first honest thing you've said all morning," Kevin said gently.

Wesley let out a breath he hadn't realized he was holding.

"I thought stepping away would fix everything," he said. "The retreat, the break, the time off. But the truth is, I don't know that I ever figured out how to come back. Not really."

Kevin leaned forward, elbows on the table.

"You don't need all the answers today. But don't bulldoze yourself into another burnout cycle just because the machine wants you moving."

He stood, gathering papers.

"And don't mistake momentum for meaning."

At the door, Kevin paused.

"For what it's worth," he added, "I'm glad you're back. But I'm even gladder you're asking the right questions this time."

When he left, the silence returned. Not peaceful. Not suffocating. Just reflective.

Wesley stared at the color-coded cities lining the calendar. It used to thrill him. Now it looked like distance measured in days. A life built on movement that suddenly felt like standing still.

He closed his eyes, pressing his palms flat against the table.

He wasn't running anymore.

But he wasn't sure he wanted to sprint either.

For the first time, he let himself sit in the uncertainty.

Forty-Six

THE KNOCK CAME JUST after nine. Sutton froze mid-step, her heart tightening before she even reached the door.

When she opened it, Graham stood there with his hands deep in his pockets, eyes shadowed. The air between them shifted immediately, a tension that felt both inevitable and unbearable.

"Hey," she said softly, stepping aside.

"Hey." His tone was polite but guarded as he crossed the threshold.

She motioned toward the couch, and they sat close, but not quite. Silence settled between them, broken only by the faint sounds of the city beyond the windows.

"Thanks for coming," she began, her voice tentative.

Graham leaned forward, elbows on his knees.

"I figured we needed to talk."

She nodded, forcing herself to meet his eyes.

"We do."

She hesitated, fingers worrying at the hem of her sweater.

"I've been thinking a lot about us. About everything."

He didn't look away.

"And?"

"I want this," she said, her voice trembling but sincere. "I want us. I know things have been strained, but I'm trying."

Graham's jaw tightened slightly. "I don't doubt that you care about me," he said quietly. "But this isn't just about effort, Sutton. It's about trust."

He shook his head slowly. "My world, my work, is built around control. Planning. Fixing things before they fall apart. But with you, I don't want that. I want to feel like I can breathe. Like I don't have to guard myself."

His voice caught.

"When I saw those photos of you and Wesley, and then learned you'd been talking to him without telling me, that crushed me."

Sutton's eyes filled.

"I didn't mean to hide it," she whispered. "I just didn't want to make it into something it wasn't. Wesley and I are just trying to be friends."

Graham exhaled steadily, but the sound carried pain.

"Maybe. But it mattered enough that you kept it from me. And if it truly meant nothing, you wouldn't have."

She flinched at the truth in it.

"I was trying to protect what we had, not destroy it."

The room fell still, the kind of silence that made every breath sound louder.

Finally, Sutton spoke.

"You matter to me, Graham. You do. I care about what we have. I just..." She trailed off, unable to finish.

He nodded once, sadness in the motion.

"The old me might have fought for this," he said quietly. "But the new me knows you have to be sure. I won't be someone's second choice. Not the safe one. Not the for now."

Tears slid down her cheeks.

"You're not a placeholder. I never saw you that way."

Graham's voice softened, though his eyes were glassy.

"Then tell me. Are you completely over him?"

Her lips parted, but no sound came.

Her silence was answer enough.

He nodded again, slower this time.

"I told you I'd wait if you needed time. But that was before everything changed. Before I realized waiting isn't the same as being chosen. I wanted to build something real with you, but you can't build anything solid when part of your heart belongs somewhere else."

Sutton's breath caught. The words landed like a truth she'd known but never dared to say aloud.

"Graham," she whispered, her voice shaking. "Please don't give up on us."

He looked at her, affection and grief tangled in his eyes.

"I'm not giving up," he said softly. "I'm letting go. I deserve someone who's all in. And so do you."

He hesitated for a moment, as if committing her face to memory, then stepped closer. His hand rose to her cheek, a final gesture of tenderness that only deepened the ache between them.

"You're an incredible woman," he said. "I hope you find what you're looking for. I just wish it could have been me."

He pressed a lingering kiss to her forehead, then turned toward the door.

She watched him go, her body rooted in place, each step widening the distance between them.

It wasn't just a breakup. It was the loss of comfort, of certainty, of the life she had almost convinced herself was enough.

And deep down, she knew it had been coming all along.

Forty-Seven

Wesley was deep into the tour now, the initial jitters replaced by a formality that had become second nature.

Backstage at a packed venue in Atlanta, anticipation thrummed through the air. Crew members darted between cords and speakers, voices overlapping as lights flashed overhead. The sharp tang of metal and sweat mixed with the electricity of a crowd waiting to erupt.

Amid the frenzy, Wesley stood steady. Clad in his signature white T-shirt and dark jeans, he adjusted his earpiece and mic with practiced ease. Whatever charge ran through him now wasn't nerves but the raw exhilaration of stepping onto the stage where he felt most alive.

"Five minutes, Wesley!" his stage manager called, weaving past with a clipboard.

"Got it," he replied, nodding to the band.

Fist bumps all around, the familiar ritual grounding him. He drew one slow breath and let the moment settle.

The lights dimmed. The crowd roared as the opening video flared across the giant screens. Wesley stepped through the curtain, swallowed by the blinding white of the spotlight.

As the first chords rang out, adrenaline surged through him.

From high-energy anthems to stripped-down ballads, he moved effortlessly through the set, commanding the stage with a presence that made everything else disappear. When the final notes of the encore dissolved into the roar of the crowd, he stepped forward, voice warm and steady.

"Thank you, Atlanta! You've been incredible!"

After the show, the noise faded, but the adrenaline still raced through his veins. The team's congratulations blurred around him. A golf cart whisked him to his SUV, and finally he was alone.

He slumped into the leather seat, sweat cooling on his skin. His phone buzzed with notifications, but his eyes lingered on one familiar name near the top of his messages.

Arya.

Her last text: ***So proud of you. Call when you can.***

Three days old.

He'd answered with a simple thumbs-up emoji, and that was the end. Their conversations had dwindled lately, swallowed by time zones and obligations. What once felt easy now felt like work. He told himself it was the distance, but deep down he knew better.

What they had was already fading, long before the world would notice.

On impulse, he opened the message thread and snapped a quick selfie. He flashed a peace sign, a grin, the afterglow of the show still written across his face, and hit send.

Show #8 done. Let's chat soon. It's been too long.

He watched the message deliver, then leaned his head against the window as city lights flickered past.

Another night. Another city.

***

Sutton was already half-asleep when her phone buzzed beside her.

She squinted at the screen, her heart skipping when she saw Wesley's name.

The photo appeared first. He stood there in his post-show glow, peace sign raised, grin wide and unguarded. She couldn't help but smile, even with the ache she still felt from losing Graham.

Below it, his message read:

Show #8 done. Let's chat soon; it's been too long.

She typed back before she could think too much about it.

Another city you've graced with your presence and left some of your heart in.

His reply came almost instantly.

Maybe one day you'll come see the show.

You're not in NYC for months, she answered. ***It'll be next year before I get the chance.***

Any show you want, **he wrote.** ***Let me know. Bring some friends. It would be cool to see you.***

Sutton stared at the screen, the words hovering like a dare. Support between friends should have been simple, but deep down she knew it wasn't.

She exhaled and opened another thread, typing impulsively.

What do you think about seeing Wesley on one of his tour dates?

Brynn's reply came seconds later.

When? NY or LA?

Sutton pulled up the schedule Wesley had sent months ago, scrolling through city after city until one caught her eye.

Miami next weekend.

Within moments, Brynn was calling.

"Wait, are you serious?" she laughed, her voice warm and incredulous through the speaker.

"I am," Sutton admitted with a smile. "Thought it might be fun. What do you think?"

Brynn's voice softened.

"Miami sounds amazing. We could make it a couple's trip if I bring Alexander."

"Wesley and I are not a couple," Sutton said quickly, maybe too quickly. "I'm supporting him as a friend. That's it. We're not going there again."

"Uh-huh." Brynn's tone made it clear she didn't believe it for a second. "Sure, whatever helps you sleep at night," she teased. "Anyway, yes, let's do it."

"Perfect," Sutton said, relief and excitement threading together inside her. "Wesley said to bring friends."

Brynn considered that for a moment.

"So are we firmly in the just-friends camp here, or should I be packing tissues for emotional fallout?"

Sutton laughed despite herself.

"It's nothing like that. He texted me and it felt completely casual. No strings."

"If you say so," Brynn teased. "Just make sure you know what you want before jumping into something that might start feeling cozy again for all the wrong reasons."

"I know," Sutton said, though part of her wasn't sure she did.

Brynn sighed, gentler now.

"Then let's make it a trip. You need one."

When the call ended, Sutton typed a short message to Wesley.

How's next weekend sound?

His reply came almost instantly.

For what? My show?

She smiled as she typed.

Where else would we want to be? Oh, and by "we," I mean Brynn, Alexander, and me.

Absolutely! he wrote back a moment later. ***Bring whoever you want. Can't wait to see you.***

This wasn't about old feelings, she told herself. It was about friendship, music, and fun.

At least, that was the story she believed.

Forty-Eight

THE HUMID MIAMI AIR buzzed with energy as Brynn, Alexander, and Sutton hurried through the streets around Hard Rock Stadium. Their delayed flight had turned arrival into a race against time, leaving Sutton no space to sort through the swirl of emotions building inside her. Neon lights reflected off damp asphalt, the bass of distant music rolling through the warm night.

"Come on, move it!" Brynn called over her shoulder, half-laughing, half-panicked. "We're going to miss his opening!"

Sutton's heart raced, and not just from the sprint. The thought of seeing Wesley in his world sent a wave of nerves she hadn't expected. Clutching her phone, she scanned for messages from his manager, Kevin.

When they reached the security gate, the scale of the crowd hit her. Thousands of faces lit with excitement, voices blending into one living roar. At last she spotted Kevin waving near a checkpoint, passes in hand.

"You made it!" he greeted, handing them over. "I was starting to think you'd miss the whole thing."

"Thanks," Sutton said, breathless but relieved as she slipped the lanyard over her neck.

Inside, the lights cut out suddenly and a roar swept through the stadium. Then an explosion of sound.

Wesley stepped into the light, guitar slung low, the rhythm of the crowd rising to meet him.

Sutton froze.

For a heartbeat it wasn't the global star she saw. It was him.

Every lyric, every movement carried the same magnetic ease she remembered, the same presence that once pulled her in without effort.

Toward the end of the show, the stage softened. Wesley stepped forward, his voice carrying through the stadium.

"This next song is special to me," he said. "Love isn't just about being together. Sometimes it's letting go so the other person can thrive. This is for anyone who's loved deeply, let go willingly, and grown because of it."

The crowd quieted. Brynn's hand closed gently around Sutton's arm.

Then came the first notes of *Sacrifice*.

Thousands of phone flashlights flickered to life, a galaxy of trembling stars. Sutton's throat tightened. Hearing it live felt different. Every word carried a closeness that made the stadium disappear.

I gave you my heart, I gave us more days,

But sometimes love's not enough to sustain.

Her vision blurred. Pride, ache, and something dangerously close to longing tangled inside her.

When the final chord faded, the crowd erupted. Wesley bowed his head, breathing hard, before lifting his gaze again to the ocean of light before him.

Sutton clapped with everyone else, but the world around her seemed to narrow, the roar of the stadium fading until only the echo of the song remained.

***

The backstage corridors were a swirl of organized chaos. Roadies rolled cases, stagehands shouted over clattering equipment, and the air carried sweat and lingering adrenaline. Kevin led the group through the narrow maze, his headset crackling with chatter.

"Watch your step. This place turns into an obstacle course after a show," he called back.

Sutton smiled faintly, the surrounding noise oddly comforting. It felt like stepping into Wesley's world, chaotic but alive.

When they reached the dressing room, Kevin knocked once before pushing the door open. Inside, laughter and the faint scent of cologne and hairspray hung in the air. Wesley turned from the mirror, his grin cutting through the fatigue. His eyes lit up when he saw them.

"There's everyone," he said, surprise and warmth mixing in his voice.

Before Sutton could reply, he crossed the room in three strides and pulled her into a hug, lifting her slightly off the ground. She laughed, the sound light and genuine.

"Your show was such a blast," she said, still a little breathless.

"Don't make me blush in front of my crew," he teased, setting her down but staying close.

"Too late," one of his guitarists called out with a grin. "We're all witnesses."

Laughter rippled through the room. Brynn stepped forward with her usual flair.

"Hey, superstar, remember the rest of us exist?"

Wesley chuckled and turned to greet her and Alexander, pulling Brynn into a quick hug.

"Of course. I owe you both a drink for making it out here."

Kevin appeared again, signaling that the after-show chaos was winding down. "Restaurant's ready if you're good to go."

Brynn smirked. "I'll hold you to that. I like expensive cocktails."

Kevin appeared again, signaling that the post-show scramble was winding down.

"Restaurant's ready if you're good to go."

"Let's go. I'm starving," Wesley said, grabbing his jacket.

He glanced back at Sutton as they stepped into the hallway.

"You good?"

She smiled, appreciating the small gesture.

"I'm good."

***

The restaurant sat on a quiet corner of the city, dimly lit and filled with soft jazz. The staff had set aside a private table near the back, half hidden by hanging ferns and the low glow of candlelight.

Plates arrived in slow succession: grilled snapper, citrus salad, truffle pasta, and chilled wine. Kevin shared stories about near disasters on past tours. Brynn kept everyone laughing with quick, irreverent jokes. Alexander offered thoughtful observations about the set design and visuals Wesley had brought to life on stage.

Wesley seemed relaxed, lighter than Sutton remembered. He gestured animatedly as he talked about the new album, about finding rhythm on the road again, about rediscovering what he loved about performing. Every so often his eyes drifted to Sutton. Quick, unguarded glances that lingered just long enough for her to notice.

When Brynn stepped away to take a call, Alexander leaned back in his chair, an amused grin tugging at his mouth.

"You know," he murmured to Sutton, glancing between her and Wesley, "I've never seen two people say so much without actually talking."

Sutton laughed, quick and easy. Too quick for how suddenly her pulse had jumped.

Brynn returned just in time to catch the end of it.

"You two are trouble," she teased, sliding back into her seat with a knowing smile.

When the meal finally wound down, dessert plates sat empty and the second bottle of wine was nearly gone. Most of the band and Kevin had already headed out.

Brynn stifled a yawn.

"Okay, I'm officially done. Old married couple bedtime," she announced, nudging Alexander.

He stood, stretching with an easy smile.

"You two behave," he said, tipping his chin toward Sutton and Wesley before leaving with Brynn.

"I'm glad you came," Wesley said quietly as he rose from the table.

"Me too." Sutton smiled. "Thanks for inviting us. And for the tickets."

He looked at her, his smile widening.

"One of the most memorable shows of the tour so far."

Sutton's smile softened.

"You make it sound like I was part of the show."

He laughed softly.

"In some ways, you always are."

A pause settled between them. Then he nodded toward the street.

"I'm not tired yet. Any chance you'd come back to the hotel? We could talk, maybe have a nightcap?"

She hesitated, caught between reason and instinct.

"Just to unwind," he added quickly, reading her silence. "No pressure, I promise."

"Sure," she said finally, her voice steady despite the quickening in her chest.

Forty-Nine

The hotel suite still held the echo of the city below. Music and laughter drifted faintly through the glass, but inside the room was still.

Wesley shrugged off his jacket and tossed his keycard onto the counter.

"Drink?" he asked, crossing to the minibar.

Sutton shook her head with a small smile.

"No, thanks. I think I've hit my limit for the night."

He poured himself one anyway, something amber.

Sutton moved to the window, her reflection a soft outline against the skyline.

"You look tired," she said.

"Tour life. It's like living in motion. One city to the next. Half the time you forget what time zone you're in."

She glanced back at him.

"But you love it, don't you?"

"Parts of it," he admitted. "The stage, the connection. That part is real. Everything around it..." He rolled the glass slowly between his hands. "It wears you down. Some nights I feel like I'm performing the version of me people expect, not the person I actually am."

Sutton turned to face him fully.

"That sounds lonely."

"It is," he said simply. "Even with all those people watching."

She sank onto the couch, curling one leg beneath her.

"You've always carried everyone else's expectations. It's what made you incredible. And what almost broke you."

He met her gaze, a faint smile touching his mouth.

"You always knew how to say the hard things without making them hurt."

Sutton shrugged lightly.

"Someone had to."

For a while neither spoke. Wesley sat across from her, elbows on his knees, expression thoughtful.

"I keep asking myself what all of it means," he said at last. "The shows, the fame, the chaos. It's supposed to feel like purpose, but sometimes it just feels like noise. Like I'm chasing something that doesn't even exist anymore."

Sutton's voice softened.

"Maybe the chasing isn't the problem. Maybe it's what you're chasing."

Silence settled again.

Then Wesley spoke, almost absently.

"Can I ask you something?"

She nodded.

"Why did you come?"

Sutton blinked.

"Because you invited me to your show," she said with a small smile. "And I wanted to support you."

He shook his head.

"No. Why did you come here tonight?"

She didn't answer right away. Her gaze drifted to the carpet. The truth was she didn't really know.

Wesley looked up, steady now.

"Selfishly, I asked because I wanted to see you."

Her breath caught.

"Then selfishly," she said quietly, "I wanted to see you too."

They both smiled. Small. Careful. Whatever they were admitting didn't have to mean more than that.

Her throat tightened.

"Wesley..."

He leaned back, eyes tracing the ceiling before returning to her.

"How are you and Arya?" she asked.

He sighed.

"We're technically still together. But we barely talk anymore. She's busy. I'm gone most of the time. I think we both see what's coming."

Sutton looked away.

"I'm sorry."

He shook his head.

"Don't be. She's great. Just bad timing."

Sutton hesitated.

"Graham and I broke up," she said quietly. "A few weeks ago. I'd rather not get into it."

For a moment Wesley didn't react.

Inside, something lifted in his chest before he could stop it. Relief. Sharp and immediate.

He pushed it down.

"I'm sorry to hear that," he said, keeping his voice even. "I thought you two were good together."

Sutton studied him for half a beat, then a small smirk tugged at her mouth.

"That was a terrible lie."

Wesley huffed a quiet breath, caught.

"Okay. Maybe not my best acting."

Her smile faded as she exhaled slowly.

"While we're being honest tonight. We can't go down this road again, Wesley."

"I know," he said quietly. "That's not what I want."

"Then what do you want?"

He thought for a moment.

"To be in your life without breaking it again."

The air seemed to leave her lungs.

"That's a hard promise."

"I know."

They sat with the truth of it.

After a moment Sutton stood, smoothing the hem of her dress.

"I should go."

He rose too.

"Yeah."

At the door she paused.

"You'll figure it out, Wesley. Whatever it is you're chasing. Or maybe what you're meant to stop chasing."

He smiled faintly.

"You always believed I could."

"I still do."

She opened the door.

He watched her step into the hallway, the light catching her shoulders before the door closed behind her.

The soft click echoed through the suite.

Wesley set his drink aside and looked out at the skyline. From up here the world looked enormous and loud.

For the first time, he wondered if the life he had built was too big for him to hear himself in.

***

Four weeks had passed since Sutton's whirlwind trip to Florida.

Back in New York, the shift from autumn to winter was unmistakable. Bare trees lined the streets, their frost-dusted branches stretching upward like charcoal sketches. Strings of lights wrapped storefronts in warm gold, though the glow did little to soften the bite in the air. The city moved with its usual urgency, but Sutton found herself craving something slower.

The scent of roasted chestnuts mixed with fresh coffee as she moved through the crowds, her thoughts drifting.

Wesley lingered at the edge of her mind, like a melody half remembered yet impossible to ignore.

Since Miami, things between them had changed. They spoke less often now. A quiet distance threaded through their conversations. His tour pushed him across time zones while Sutton buried herself in deadlines, gallery work, and the rush of the holidays. The connection they had rediscovered felt fragile, stretched thin between two lives moving in different directions.

Her phone buzzed.

Sutton smiled despite herself.

She snapped a quick photo of her tea and blanket and sent it back with a playful caption about winter chaos in New York.

These small exchanges had become their rhythm. A way to stay close without touching the deeper places that might unravel them.

She missed their late night talks, the easy honesty they once shared. But neither of them seemed ready to open that door again.

For now, this was enough.

That evening she curled into the couch with a mug warming her hands while she talked with Brynn about their annual winter trip.

"I can't believe it's almost Christmas again," Sutton said, shaking her head. "This year has been... a lot."

"No kidding," Brynn laughed. "At least we have the trip to look forward to. You deserve a break."

Sutton smiled.

"We all do."

There was a pause before Brynn spoke again, softer this time.

"It's wild to think it's been almost a year since you and Wesley met."

Sutton's gaze drifted to a photo on her shelf. A candid shot from Miami. She and Wesley mid laugh, both of them unguarded.

She smiled faintly.

"Yeah," she said quietly. "Hard to believe."

Brynn launched into restaurant ideas and excursion plans, but Sutton's thoughts wandered.

She pictured Wesley on tour. City after city. Bright lights and louder applause.

Their lives felt like parallel lines. Touching occasionally before pulling apart again.

Still, she couldn't ignore the pull between them.

Persistent. Uncertain. Impossible to fully leave behind.

After the call ended, Sutton stayed on the couch, her tea cooling in her hands as she looked out at the frosted skyline.

Winter had always been her favorite season.

Not for the cold.

But for the pause it offered.

A chance to take stock.

To reflect.

To breathe.

Fifty

THE STAGE LIGHTS HAD dimmed. The applause was already fading into memory.

For the first time in months, Wesley was home for Thanksgiving. The tour was on pause until the new year.

When he stepped into his parents' house, the familiar rhythm of it all settled around him. The scent of baked pies drifted from the kitchen. His parents moved easily around each other, the quiet choreography of people who had spent decades sharing a life.

For the first time in a long while, he felt calm.

Months on the road had made him crave something the stage could never give him. Something that couldn't be measured in ticket sales or charts.

Something steady. Real.

That night at dinner, Wesley found himself watching his parents more than eating. The way his father refilled his mother's water without asking. The quick smiles they traded across the table. The small, practiced gestures that held their lives together.

After the meal, he stayed behind to dry dishes with his mother.

She glanced at him over her shoulder.

"You've been quiet tonight," she said. "What's on your mind?"

He hesitated.

"You and Dad. How did you know? That he was the one?"

Her smile softened.

"If you're asking that," she said gently, "I think you already know your answer. Who is she?"

Wesley laughed under his breath. There was no point pretending.

He told her about Sutton. About their past. About the friendship they had tried to rebuild and the feelings that kept resurfacing no matter how far apart they drifted.

His mother listened without interrupting.

When he finished, she wiped her hands on a towel and leaned against the counter.

"Love is complicated, Wesley. Anyone who tells you it's simple hasn't lived it. It takes work. Compromise. Two people choosing each other again and again."

He stared down at the dish in his hands.

"I've spent so much time trying to get everything right," he said quietly. "Trying to be who everyone expected me to be. I drew these lines for myself like I was afraid to step outside them."

His mother reached for his hand.

"Then maybe it's time to stop living inside those lines," she said softly. "Redefine them. Make them yours."

Wesley went still.

Sacrifice.

The word drifted through his thoughts, the title of the song that had come to define so much of the last year.

His mother shook her head gently.

"Not sacrifice," she said. "Sacrifice means giving up something you still want. Real love isn't that. It's choosing what matters most and letting the rest fall away."

Her words stayed with him long after she left the kitchen.

Wesley stood at the window, frost beginning to lace the glass.

For months the ache in his chest had felt like loss.

Now it felt like direction.

He knew where he needed to go.

***

Sutton's apartment was quiet.

The last of Thanksgiving dinner sat scattered across the counter. The warmth of the evening had faded, replaced by the stillness of late night.

She was halfway through washing dishes when a knock sounded at the door.

Her heart jumped.

11:28 p.m.

She moved cautiously to the peephole and froze.

Wesley stood in the hallway, hands buried in his coat pockets, breath fogging the cold air.

"Wesley?" she said as she opened the door. "What are you doing here?"

"I know it's late," he said quietly. "I came straight from the airport. I needed to see you."

Something in his voice made her step aside without question.

"Is everything okay?" she asked.

He let out a tired breath.

"Always nice to see you too."

They sat on the couch with careful space between them.

Wesley leaned forward, searching for the right place to begin.

"I was home for Thanksgiving," he said. "Watching my parents. They've had hard years. But they kept choosing each other."

Sutton tilted her head.

"You're not about to tell me you're proposing to Arya, are you?"

He laughed softly.

"No. Arya and I ended things."

Her eyes widened.

"You did?"

"It wasn't sudden. I told you in Miami I felt it coming. She's incredible, but we were moving in different directions. It stopped feeling fair to pretend otherwise."

Sutton nodded slowly.

"I've been thinking a lot since then," he continued. "About my life. About what I've been chasing."

His eyes lifted to hers.

"I used to think the stage was home. The travel. The spotlight. But that's not the part I love most."

"What is?"

"Writing. Creating. The connection behind the music."

He paused.

"After this tour, I'm done living on the road."

Her brow lifted.

"Done?"

"I want to write. For myself. For other artists. Maybe play smaller venues once in a while. But I want something rooted."

He shifted slightly closer.

"It means I'm done chasing horizons."

His voice dropped.

"I want mornings that matter. Evenings that last."

He met her eyes.

"And I want them with you."

Sutton blinked quickly.

"I know," he said softly. "It's a lot. But I've spent months trying to move on. I can't. And I don't want to."

Tears filled her eyes.

"We've been here before," she whispered. "What if we fall apart again?"

"We won't," he said. "Because I'm not asking to go back. I'm asking to start something new."

The words settled between them.

"I know what I want this time," he continued. "The spotlight will fade eventually. I'm ready for that."

Sutton wiped at her cheek.

"A different path," she said quietly.

Wesley smiled.

"The one we didn't take before."

The air between them shifted.

"I love you," Sutton said softly. "I never stopped."

Wesley exhaled, the tension leaving him all at once. He cupped her face and kissed her.

It began gently, then deepened with everything they had spent months holding back.

When they pulled apart, their foreheads rested together.

"This feels right," he whispered.

"It finally does," she said.

Outside, the city glowed against the winter sky.

Inside, they sat together in the stillness they had once been too afraid to face.

The lines of their past softened.

And in their place was something new.

Not the love they once tried to hold on to.

But the one they chose to build together.

Epilogue

Snow drifted softly from the charcoal-gray sky as Sutton stepped outside Brynn's cabin, fresh powder crunching beneath her boots in the still winter night. Wrapped in her favorite cream pea coat, she drew in the crisp air, a familiar thrill rising in her chest as she made her way toward Tati's patio.

Every year their annual winter tradition seemed to carry a little more history.

Tati's patio had once again transformed into a winter wonderland. Lights glowed warmly overhead, and snow-dusted branches shimmered as flakes fell through the air. Guests huddled beneath blankets, their laughter mingling with the soft music and the flicker of candlelight.

Sutton paused for a moment, taking it in.

It felt like coming home.

Cassie, Zoe, Marcus, and Peter were gathered around the table. They brightened when they saw her, rising for hugs and cheerful greetings. Sutton laughed as they pulled her into their circle, her heart swelling with affection for the friends who had become family.

When she reached Brynn, a familiar arm slipped around her waist.

"Sorry I'm late," came Wesley's voice behind her.

She turned instantly, smiling.

His timing reminded her of the first night they had met a year ago, except this time there was no uncertainty. Only the easy confidence of two people who had finally found their way back to each other.

"You're here," Sutton said softly.

She kissed him, a simple greeting that carried the quiet weight of everything they had built since.

Wesley settled beside her, their hands finding each other beneath the table, fingers intertwining as naturally as breathing.

Conversation flowed easily around them.

At one point Marcus mentioned, almost casually, "Did you hear about Graham? He's living abroad now. Consulting for some venture firm. Copenhagen, I think. Sounds like he's doing well."

Sutton glanced toward the falling snow.

"I'm glad," she said, and she meant it.

There was no ache in the thought now. Only gratitude for what had been and for the way they had both moved forward.

Later, as the candles burned low and music drifted through the air, Wesley leaned closer.

"You know," he murmured, his voice meant only for her, "coming back here with you feels like home."

Sutton squeezed his hand.

"Full circle," she whispered. "In the best way."

And this time, they weren't living inside the old lines anymore.

They were redefining them together.

Also by

S. Brianne

Unconventional Lines

Book Two of the Lines Duet

Coming Fall/Winter 2026

Turn the page for a sneak peek...

Sneak Peek

Prologue of

Unconventional Lines

Prologue

SUMMER 2005

The same paragraph had been sitting open in Brynn's lap for nearly ten minutes.

Not because the book was boring.

Because every few minutes, laughter drifted across the lake.

The late afternoon sun skimmed the water, turning it gold as pine trees stretched long shadows along the shoreline. The air smelled of warm grass and sunscreen, while cicadas buzzed lazily in the summer heat.

A new family had moved into the house down the road.

She hadn't learned much about them yet.

Only that they were loud.

Her eyes drifted toward the dock.

Three teenagers stood at the edge of the water. The shorter boy shoved the tallest one with both hands, sending him stumbling sideways before he caught himself at the last second.

The girl beside him laughed so hard she had to grab his arm to stay upright.

A second later, the tall boy wrapped an arm around her shoulders and shoved the shorter one into the lake instead.

His triumphant grin carried all the way across the water.

Brynn shook her head and looked back at her book.

She still didn't turn the page.

"Brynnnn!"

Her mother's voice drifted through the screen door.

"Time to get ready! Country club tonight."

Brynn closed the book with a quiet thud.

Between the new neighbors and another evening of polite conversations she'd already had a hundred times, the peaceful summer she'd been counting on was disappearing faster than she'd expected.

***

The country club sparkled as it always did. Polished marble, crystal chandeliers, and conversations carried through practiced smiles.

Her parents thrived here.

They spoke the language of investments, connections, and futures that seemed planned years in advance.

Brynn smiled when expected, nodded when spoken to, and counted the minutes until she could leave.

This life had never felt like hers.

The one bright spot was her friend, Bradley.

He stood behind the bar, sleeves rolled to his forearms, lining up wine glasses while dark hair fell across his forehead.

He moved with an easy confidence that never seemed performative.

Like none of this impressed him.

It was just a summer job.

Eventually, he'd move on.

Brynn leaned against the cool marble.

"Parents' night again?" he asked, stacking the last glass.

"You know it."

"Lucky you."

She smiled.

Bradley always found something to polish when the room grew loud.

A bottle.

A glass.

The counter.

Anything to keep one foot outside conversations he had no interest in joining.

"How've you been?" she asked.

"Same."

He shrugged.

"Saving. Planning."

That was always his answer.

Never where.

Never when.

Later, after the crowd had thinned, he pulled a folded receipt from his pocket and smoothed it across the bar.

"This is Lisbon," he said, tapping one corner of the sketch.

"If I left today, this is where I'd start."

Brynn leaned closer.

"You always say that."

"And one day I'll mean it."

He smiled, almost to himself.

He talked about leaving the way most people talked about retirement.

Not as a dream.

As something inevitable.

She liked listening to him.

Not because she wanted the same things.

Because he made the world feel bigger.

When her parents wandered back toward the bar, Bradley folded the receipt and slipped it into his pocket.

The conversation ended as easily as it had started.

That was the thing about Bradley.

Nothing ever felt complicated.

Their conversations picked up where they'd left off each summer and ended just as naturally when August did.

He never asked for more than she was willing to give.

Maybe that was why she liked being around him.

Maybe it was because, even then, she knew how the story ended.

One summer she'd come back.

He'd be gone.

And life would keep moving.

***

The next afternoon, the heat settled over Main Street like a heavy blanket.

Brynn headed toward Jack's Creamery, already thinking about a double scoop of mint chocolate chip.

She didn't see them until they burst out of the alley.

"Theo, watch out!"

The girl grabbed the shorter boy's arm just before he barreled into Brynn.

She stumbled back, her pulse jumping.

Then she recognized him.

The tall boy from the dock.

Up close, his features were sharper than she'd realized.

His expression settled on her with easy curiosity.

"I'm okay," she said, brushing a strand of hair behind her ear. "I think we live on the same street. Blue house down the road. I saw you guys at the lake."

His grin appeared slowly.

"I'm Marcus."

He nodded toward the boy beside him.

"This is my brother, Theo."

Then toward the girl.

"And Maddie. Theo's girlfriend."

Brynn slipped her hands into her pockets.

"How old are you?"

"I'm sixteen," Maddie answered. "Theo's fifteen, and Marcus is... what? Eighteen?"

"Seventeen," Marcus corrected.

His grin didn't disappear.

"And you?" Theo asked.

"Fifteen."

Brynn hesitated for half a second.

"I was headed to Jack's Creamery. You guys want to come?"

"Absolutely," Maddie said.

The boys exchanged a quick look, then fell into step beside her as though the invitation had already been accepted.

By the end of the afternoon, Brynn knew they were from Florida and that the house down the road had been in Marcus and Theo's family for years.

She learned Theo talked faster whenever he got excited.

Maddie filled every silence before it had a chance to settle.

And Marcus listened.

Two weeks passed before Maddie went back to Florida with her parents.

After that, things shifted without anyone acknowledging it.

The space beside Brynn filled easily.

Marcus was usually the reason everyone stayed a little longer.

He teased Theo until he rolled his eyes, exaggerated stories until Brynn laughed, and somehow made ordinary afternoons feel worth remembering.

Most evenings ended on the dock.

Theo narrated every skipped stone like he was calling the championship round of a sporting event.

Marcus usually started it, daring him to beat a record he'd just invented.

Other nights, Theo headed inside first.

Those evenings settled into something quieter.

Marcus stretched out beside her on the dock, hands behind his head, asking questions no one else ever thought to ask.

He never rushed her answers.

When she stopped to think, he waited.

They talked about music.

School.

College.

The places they wanted to see someday.

Sometimes they talked until conversation simply ran out.

Neither of them seemed bothered by the silence that followed.

Later, Brynn wouldn't remember every conversation.

She'd remember looking for Marcus first.

If Theo walked down to the dock alone, she'd ask where Marcus was.

If Marcus showed up without Theo, she'd glance toward the house, expecting him to follow.

Somewhere along the way, the four of them had become three.

Then, quietly, they became two.

She couldn't have known it then, but some people don't enter your life all at once.

They become part of it so gradually that you never notice the exact moment they stay.

www.ingramcontent.com/pod-product-compliance
Lightning Source LLC
LaVergne TN
LVHW090552110826
845146LV00001B/107

* 9 7 9 8 9 9 9 2 0 9 6 1 0 *